Tavern's Corner
In the Adirondacks

Dan Gillman

North Country Books
Utica, New York

Tavern's Corner
In the Adirondacks

by
Dan Gillman

Copyright © 2000

ISBN 0-925168-77-7

Cover art and illustrations by Jane Burns
Cover Design by Sheri Amsel

NORTH COUNTRY BOOKS, INC.
311 Turner Street
Utica, New York 13501

Contents

Pathfinder   1

One Man's Scent   14

Sneaky Pete   23

The Fly, The Fish, and The Foolish   42

McQuiren's Boarding House   52

The Yankees Fan and A Number Six Fly   63

The Buying of the Old Mill House   70

A Path Less Trod   75

Old Ben   80

Cabin Fever   90

The Witch of Tupper Lake   96

The Woodsman   110

Introduction

In the heart of the Adirondack Mountains lies a small, town-like place called Tavern's Corner. Tavern's Corner doesn't have many residents but it makes up for that with the character of the people who do live there. Their simple, common sense philosophy, their love of nature and the great outdoors, mixed with life's ironic humor make for some pretty interesting stories. If you consider yourself the outdoor type or just enjoy a quiet chuckle, I think you will enjoy reading *Tavern's Corner*.

PATHFINDER

Terrence Nesmond was known as Nesy, a nickname given to him in grade school. Now, at thirty-three, it was just his name. His mom, wife, friends, everyone called him Nesy. Nesy never thought much about it although he always introduced himself as Terrence. Nesy was a city boy of sorts. He lived in Eastchester, New York where he was raised. He attended private school and college, and then followed up with law school. Now he was a small peg in a large law firm slowly making his way up the corporate ladder.

Nesy had been traveling North on I-87. After

getting off at Exit 30 for Keene Valley, he hung a 'ralf' and two 'louies,' marking his jumping off point into the heart of the Adirondack Mountains. One month of careful planning had gone into this trip. He had read every catalog he could snatch to find any gear that might prove vital. He now felt he was completely prepared.

It was eleven thirty in the morning and Nesy was hungry. A large brunch was in order. Perhaps he could find a place to eat and get directions to a rugged, desolate spot for hiking; a place to go forth and conquer, alone with nature. It was a corny thought and it made him snort and choke in laughter.

Ten minutes later Nesy was passing an obscure little building. The sign read, "TAVERN — food and drink, City Folk Welcome." A well-calculated five-point turn brought the red Range Rover in front of the establishment. He assumed the inside would have a rustic-inn look, maybe even with a large buffet in progress. Wishful thinking. In reality, it was dark with streaks of light from the windows showing thick dust suspended in the air. The left side of the room was all bar with unfamiliar bottles of liquor and large jars of yellow liquid. Some contained eggs and others what looked like large hot dogs. They reminded him of specimen jars.

In the corner of the room stood a fireplace with low-burning embers. An old man with deep wrinkles sat in a rocking chair, staring intently into the hearth. His ragged hat hung from the corner of the rocker. When the old man slowly rose to add a piece of wood to the fire, Nesy noticed his knotted, swollen hands. The pain of the man's arthritis was too much and he dropped the wood chunk with a low moan. Slowly he bent to pick up the wood again, but Nesy beat him to it. Nesy plopped the log on the fire, then poked it until the flames grew high. He gently lowered the old man into his rocker. The old man stared at Nesy, but never said a word. Nesy compulsively stared back at the old man's raven black eyes. He could not look away no matter how hard he tried. Very slowly the old man's eyes settled back on the fire. When he reached for the small table next to the rocker, Nesy moved it closer. Resting on the table was a small wooden box that contained several hand-made smoking pipes. The man took one out, smelled the end of it, and caressed it between his thumb and fingers.

Meanwhile, voices coming from a doorway at the back of the bar distracted Nesy. As he approached the bar, three men tumbled out of the doorway followed by a Ninja warrior armed with a broom. The "Ninja" was a woman in her seventies wearing a light blue full-length dress and checkered apron. The broom moved with lightning speed. Quick jabs followed long roundhouse swings, all of which hit home with solid thuds. Straw bristles filled the air. The three men called her Ma, saying they were only trying to help.

"I don't need your help nor the mess. Set yourselves down and I'll feed you when it's ready!" she yelled.

All wore smiles until their heads turned in Nesy's direction. The smiles changed to blank stares. Nesy took a deep swallow, finding it hard to get his words out.

"Saw the sign, missed breakfast. I find myself hungry. If it's not too much trouble could I get some poached eggs, toast, dark bacon, half a grapefruit, O.J., and a tall milk?"

Luke and Earl sat on the barstools while Jed lingered behind the bar next to Ma. Ma finally smiled, nodded her head, and disappeared through the doorway.

Nesy felt more than a little uncomfortable. Only now he noticed he was dripping with sweat, mostly because of the flannel one-piece long johns he had on. (He mentally said he would be glad later. He'd read in the catalog that it sometimes gets surprisingly chilly in late April.) The dead silence and blank stares did not help his predicament.

Nesy noticed earlier that all three men were wearing Yankee baseball caps, so he decided to make conversation. Unfortunately, he said the wrong thing:

"How about those Yankees! Do you think they'll be able to go the distance this year? The Yankees slam dunking the World Series the way they did last year has created some very expensive egos. I hope they can pull it back together, forget about their super stardom, and play ball. You know Steinbrenner, that so-called team owner, won't be any kind of help."

To Luke, Earl, and Jed that was a declaration of war. Luke and Earl came off their stools as Jed leaped over the bar. Nesy didn't know what happened. One minute he was standing, the next he was a foot off the ground. Luke bent Nesy's left arm behind his back. Earl had one paw around his neck and the other on his right wrist. In terrible slow motion Nesy was being levitated toward the door.

Nesy heard a long bear-like growl that echoed off the walls and turned all heads. Time froze. The old man stood very tall with the reflection of the flames glowing in his eyes. The three brothers became motionless. Nesy thought he saw fear in their

eyes, but quickly realized they stood still out of respect and awe of the old man. As they watched, the
man then shrank and his back hunched once again.
Feebly reaching for his chair, he sunk down with a
heavy sigh.

Everything had changed. The boys placed Nesy
on a barstool. Luke and Earl sat beside him as Jed
worked behind the bar. Four long necks sat in
front of them and Jed was talking about the Yankees.

"It's all political bull-dung," he said.

Nesy quickly agreed. Within the next thirty
minutes, ten pounds of shepherd's pie was de-
voured and eight more long necks were guzzled.
The boys were astounded by the sports facts and
statistics Nesy had at his command. They used
those to prove various points of long unsettled ar-
guments.

Before too long Nesy was on his way to a remote spot Jed suggested. He now was trying to
mentally repeat the directions Jed had given him.
Take a right where the rock ledge meets the road,
left at birch stand, stay on dirt road, and on and on
he went. Nesy could not believe he actually drove
away thanking Jed, thinking he knew where he
was going. He was lost. The dirt road abruptly
ended. Nesy looked around, shrugged his shoul-

ders, and parked the car.

His pack was an engineering marvel. He was very proud, everything was in place, and it only took four bungee cords and fifteen feet of rope to hold it together.

The sun was setting and Nesy was confident he could get a couple of miles under his belt before dark. Trails are for amateurs, he thought, and decided to save the compass reading for later. He would rely on his natural sense of direction for now. Hefting his pack to his back he immediately folded to one knee in surprise. Bracing himself against the car, Nesy rose, hoping he would loosen up eventually. After all, he had played racket ball twice a week for the last three weeks to get in shape for this trip.

A slow staggering two hundred yards later, he came to a small mountain stream where he decided to camp for the night. To lighten the load of his burdensome pack, Nesy stuffed himself with food before climbing into his bag to sleep.

The night dragged. Nesy awoke many times to weird noises and strange shadows. He stuffed himself at breakfast, figuring to lighten his load. Along the same line, he decided to leave other things behind and retrieve them on his way back. He left his new one-slice solar operated toaster, a wind-up alarm clock with a glow in the dark feature and a fifteen minute snooze button, an extra wide tree hammock with a roll up mat, an eight-piece cooking pan kit (nonstick), and particularly painful, his own concoction of peanut butter, jelly, fluffernutter, and trail mix. Oh yes, he left all the clothing he was not wearing at the time.

Leaving camp, Nesy followed the stream. He carried his pack with ease, thinking as he walked, light and mobile, this is the key. His pack was practically empty. His stomach, on the other hand, was bulging at the seams. Two hundred yards later he disposed of a roll of Tums and a canteen of water. It didn't help.

He quickly grew exhausted and couldn't understand why. Around noon he came to a waterfall where the water churned and a spray of mist was in the air. Realizing he could not hold it any longer, Nesy removed his pack, walked thirty yards and found a likely spot. Crouched in that infamous position, Nesy looked around and felt that all of Mother Nature was watching and laughing. Birds and squirrels stared at his paleness while the insect world attacked in full force. Nesy soon realized he had forgotten one vital necessity. Fifteen minutes later he was on his way. His one-piece flannel long johns were now altered to short sleeve.

Nesy wasn't exactly sure which way to go. It was time to take a compass reading and he had just the watch to do it. The watch was a gift from his dad on his sixteenth birthday. It had everything. Besides the time, date, and stopwatch, it had an alarm that played a Beatles medley, a listing of all the family birthdays, even the date and score of his senior high school basketball team championship game. (He was assistant to the coach—water boy.) The built-in compass would have worked well had Nesy held still long enough to let the needle settle.

Nesy chose North and headed toward the nearest mountain. The woods grew thick as his field of vision grew smaller and smaller. The woods seemed to be closing in on him. Panting as he swam through the thick pines, he hoped the woods would open up and let him breathe when he drew closer to the mountain.

Night came. Nesy never found the mountain. Although he was tired, he couldn't sleep. Nesy admitted to himself that he was scared and he toyed with the possibility that he might be lost. He made a large fire. One of the items he didn't leave behind was his coffeepot. When he had packed it he hadn't noticed the cord on the pot. It wasn't practical here in the woods and it smelled funny when it caught fire, but, nonetheless, the coffee tasted good.

Nesy gazed at the stars with amazement. The sky was illuminated with bright dots, some close and bright, others duller, giving the sky endless depth and silence. The silence was unlike the woods around him, which were alive with indistinguishable noises. Nesy did not remember going to sleep, but when he woke he recalled dreaming of the shadowy figure of a man kneeling on the other side of the fire, warming his hands and sipping coffee. He shrugged it off and began packing his things when he looked across the coals of the fire and, stunned, saw his coffee cup.

Soon after resuming the hike, Nesy admitted to himself that he was lost, and scared. He began jogging slowly and swallowing hard as if to fight down the fear that wanted to erupt. Even people you'd call woodsmen have gotten themselves turned around one time or another. Whether they would admit it to others later or not wasn't an important question. They would know that it doesn't take long for a little alarm to go off and an inner voice to say, get me out of here! An experienced woodsman would take a short break and then try to reason his way out. He would use his map, compass, landmarks, time of travel, or something as simple as walking towards or away from the sun. The woodsman understood that panic was his enemy.

Nesy didn't know. He was drenched in sweat and dizzy from hyperventilating. Exhaustion finally made him stop and lean against a large tree. He was still gasping for air when he noticed a thick cloud-like mist moving along the ground. In the middle of the mist it seemed as if a man was standing looking at Nesy and shaking his head. He slowly raised a hand and waved for Nesy to come over. The man turned away, took two steps, and disappeared. Nesy wasn't sure what to make of it and he could not tell exactly why, but he slowly walked off in the same direction.

Realizing it was getting dark, Nesy gathered plenty of extra firewood and made a bright fire. He finished off his pepperoni and made a large pot of coffee. There was a certain calmness in Nesy that couldn't be explained. Perhaps it was the feeling that he was not quite alone. At that thought he added wood to the fire and placed his coffee cup and pot on a rock within easy reach.

He made himself comfortable and somewhere between watching the stars and the shadows made by the fire, he dozed off.

The extraordinary events of the night were all so vivid when he woke in the morning. He remembered waking to the sound of the cup being lifted off the rock. He watched a shadowy figure across the fire pouring himself a cup of coffee from the pot. The figure appeared to be a well-aged man, although Nesy could only see a rough outline. The campfire man was wearing a checkered shirt with greenish pants and coat and an old hat tilted back on his head. He nodded his head as he raised the cup. No words were spoken. The man pulled out a pipe, lit it and seemed very content.

The two men spent the night watching clouds sweep across the moon and intermittently block out patches of stars. The campfire man buttoned his coat and raised his hands to feel the fire's heat one last time. The shadow-man looked directly at Nesy and tipped his hat as if to say thanks, then turned and vanished.

Nesy could not convince himself that it hadn't happened. He broke camp slowly, thinking about the night. Just before he left he found a row of rocks pointing across the ridge. Curious, he followed them. He found several others and by mid-afternoon he was at the waterfall and recognized instantly where he was. The car was close by and there was no need to hurry.

He lay down among the roots of a large tree and warmed his face in the sun. Looking across the pool, Nesy thought he caught a glimpse of the campfire man in the mist rising from the falls. He appeared to be drinking from the stream. He then rose, put on his hat, tilted it low, and vanished.

ONE MAN'S SCENT

Jed grinned. There was no doubt that this was the little valley Uncle had described. It was well worth going two or three miles out of the way. If hidden places still existed, this was one of them. Jed, on a solitary sightseeing and fishing expedition, stood and thought of his uncle.

Everyone knew that Uncle had "the gift." He could verbally guide you from New York to Canada, describing every river, mountain, and tree worth mentioning. Townsfolk always went to Uncle to find the best of the hidden fishing holes or long forgotten game trails on misbegotten mountains. He not only knew where these places were, but when and how to fish or hunt them. He knew which bait to use and what time of day, or night for that matter, deer would leave their swamps. He would know which pass the deer would use to climb the mountains, and whether they were looking for sweet grass, sour young tree buds, or ripened nuts.

"All things have habits, which are usually dictated by nature," he'd say.

Folks listened to Uncle—that is, if he were inclined to talk. Uncle's insights almost always led to success. Occasionally, he would ask peculiar questions such as, "What color are the leaves on the old oak at the edge of town?" He might ask how deep the snow is underneath the pines at the side yard, or note how fast the clouds have been traveling the last couple of days. If asked about rainbow trout, he might go check the thermometer that he always kept inside the rain barrel. Sometimes he is overheard mumbling to himself something like, "t'aint seen any red beetles yet, nor flyin' ants." Uncle was a knowing man.

Jed started his trip yesterday at Thirteenth Lake with a day of fishing that yielded mostly small stock trout. Jed had his heart set on catching natives, with their rainbow-like bellies and sweet, pink meat. Uncle had given him directions to a remote spot called Robinson's Swamp. Leaving Farmer's Clearing—directly south of the lake and where Jed had camped for the night—he traveled southeast, keeping Bullhead Mountain, with its slate-like walls, to his left shoulder, " 'til you see a mountain that stands all alone looking like the arch in a soldier's back at attention." This would be Chimney Mountain.

Jed recalled Uncle's words, "It has a long arm on the north side—follow it. Just before entering Chimney Pass, you'll cross the strangest little valley."

Uncle had said the valley reminded him of something mythical, almost magical, one of nature's rarities. Everything—the ground, rocks, trees—was covered with a bushy, bright green moss. The moss was full of water beads, which sparkled in the morning sun. It was beautiful. Jed was absorbing the whole scene, perhaps not paying attention to what he was doing. As Jed saw it, hindsight was greatly exaggerated, being it's usually after the fact. It's nothing more than a fancy, city folk way of calling yourself a fool.

Lying there on his back it seemed he still could hear the echo of his leg snapping. There had been a small pile of blown-down pine trees. Instead of walking around them, he tried to cross over them and wind his way through. His attention was not on the ground or the placement of his feet. He had stepped between two limbs, shifting his weight to his left foot which was on a small rock covered with moss. The moss gave way and down he went.

Jed was not one to mope or whine over a bad situation. So, after ten or twelve colorful words linked together rather quickly, Jed tried to sit up. Fifteen minutes later, he tried again, this time successfully.

Now, Jed grew up knowing that if you go into the woods, you best go relying on no one but yourself. And Jed knew which side of the tree the moss grew on.

It wasn't long before he had crawled around on his butt like a maimed spider, and had made a makeshift splint for his leg. He was thinking of taking a little nap before trying to stand when he noticed he could see his breath in the air. A couple of seconds later snow began to fall. So much for the sixty degree spring-like weather the newsman had mentioned. Jed was painfully hobbling around, looking for something to use as a crutch before snow covered the ground. At the same time, he pondered alternate job opportunities for weathermen.

Uncle had mentioned several caves in Chimney

Pass. He had named a particular one Gollum, after a character in the Hobbit books by J.R.R. Tolkien, Uncle's favorite author. The cave entrance was nothing more than a rough four by four hole in the ground. It was easy to locate because it was at the base of the largest tree in the Pass, and the Pass itself was only forty feet wide.

Jed had to crawl for the first few feet, then suddenly the tunnel entered into a large cavern. Uncle had once used it as a winter hunting camp. He had mentioned there was another entrance at the far end of the cavern.

The cave was unlike other caves of the Adirondacks. It was dry and comfortable, with a layer of loose dirt on the floor and light that somehow channeled in through the ceiling. Uncle had said something about the cave being solar heated. The outside of its walls and roof were exposed to the sun, which explained its coziness.

"Uncle was right—this place ain't bad at all," he thought.

Jed had been traveling light, just his usual small daypack. It's not how much you bring, but rather what you bring with you. He had a wool blanket, a can of peaches, a can of corn, several tea bags, and a full water jug. Yes, he could hold up for a day or two, no problem. He removed his leg brace and stripped down to his boxers to survey the damage. His leg was only slightly swollen, and although it throbbed, perhaps it wasn't a bad break after all.

Jed used his clothes as bedding beneath him and his wool blanket to cover him. Quite snug. In those brief, groggy minutes before sleep took hold, he was bothered by something. He couldn't quite place the trouble, but whatever it was made his nose twitch.

Exhausted, he slept for ten hours without stirring a muscle. He awoke slowly, not wanting to commit to getting up yet. Slowly, very slowly, a strange noise worked its way into his dream world. He could not place what that noise was, or why he was dreaming it. Realizing he was awake, opening one eye, and then the other, Jed could still hear the noise. It had to be his brothers, Jake and Earl; they were sleeping. He had heard their snores before, but they were in rare form now. How could they have found him so fast? Why hadn't they awakened him?

Peering across the cavern, his eyes were slow to focus. It took a couple minutes for him to believe what he was seeing. Lurking in the shadows on the opposite side of the cavern was a large black bear. Jed stared in disbelief. The bear was sleeping soundly. How could this be happening? More than likely the bear had spent the winter in the cave, woke up hungry and groggy from its sleep and went for a short walk. When the weather had turned bad, it must have decided to return to its cave. A bear would never be a great threat to anyone, Jed thought. They are by nature great scaredy-cats. But then, all animals are dangerous when cornered, protecting their young or wounded. Jed was trying to ponder his way out of the situation, thinking about inching his way out when his circumstance grew drastically worse.

He noticed some movement and his first thought was that the bear was awakening. Once again, it took a couple of seconds for his eyes to focus. Next to the big sow was a young cub, staring right back at him. The cub was playing with a small rock and sniffing the air, obviously trying to locate the strange scent. One cry from the cub would more than likely send his mom into a rage. The cub kicked the rock as if daring Jed to go closer. The cub sniffed constantly. When Jed also took a deep breath he was almost choked by his own smell. In the last couple of days he had really ripened.

Jed had an idea. He took his shirt and threw it toward the big sow, hoping she would smell the human scent, realize the "danger," grab her cub, and get the heck out of Dodge. Unfortunately, the young cub stood up on his hind legs, caught the shirt and proceeded to tear it to shreds. Jed tried again with his T-shirt, followed by his pants. Junior was having a great time. One of his front paws was now shoved down through a pant leg and he was doing some altering on the other.

In complete frustration Jed took off his socks and balled them together. He threw them as hard and as high as he could, trying to go over Junior's head. At the peak of the arch, the socks separated and slowly floated down. One of the socks landed directly on the sow's nose. At first she didn't even flinch. Soon she took several slow sniffs followed by several short snorts. Her eyes shot open suddenly. They rolled back so Jed could see the whites. She jumped up and immediately cuffed Junior in the buttocks with her large paw. The two of them scurried through that far entrance that Jed had not yet explored.

Jed wasted no time. He grabbed his boots and crutch and got out of there. Thirty minutes later Jed was on the trail to King's Flow. Luckily, he ran into a group of friendly hikers who were more than happy to give him a lift once they got to King's Flow. The group, being a Girl Scout Troop, had quite a first impression of Jed, wearing nothing but his boxers and boots.

Three days later Jed hobbled into the Tavern House, his leg encased in a full length cast. The ball game was on, Yanks versus the Sox. Jed made his way to the bar and took the long-neck placed in front of him.

His brother leaned over, moved Jed's crutches out of the way and said, "Bottom of the ninth, six to four, Yanks." No one asked any questions, nor did any eyes wander from the screen. In the back of the room, by the fire, sat an old man smoking his pipe smiling and quietly chuckling to himself.

SNEAKY PETE

Uncle rocked in his chair in front of the fireplace. The smell of his pipe filled the room. Jed and Nesy were sitting close by, talking about the upcoming whitewater derby. The Adirondack Hudson River Whitewater Derby was in two weeks, and they were talking strategies and schemes.

"How long has this whitewater canoe race been going on, and just how did it get started?" Nesy asked.

Uncle had cleared his throat as was his way when about to spin a yarn. Jed settled back in his chair. Nesy dropped a couple of logs on the fire, sat back, and propped up his feet.

When Uncle told a story, it was as if he was mentally rolling back through the years, like turning the pages of a thick book. Sometimes he would mention headlines from the pages, to help direct him to the proper spot.

"Of course, most people think the Hudson River Whitewater Derby became popular when that young Kennedy boy was up here. I remember it snowed that weekend, and the river was at a good pace. That weekend ended up with a whole lot of folks going for chilly spring baths. It made quite a spectacle," Uncle said.

"As far as I'm concerned, it all started back in the late thirties. The main occupation at that time was logging. The logging camps built holding pens along the Hudson River to store up their winter timber. They used the spring high water to float their logs to the local mills or to waiting trains for shipping. Finch and Pruyn, a large pulp mill corporation, was the big outfit back then. They owned the land and the trees on it. They hired various logging companies to come in and harvest the trees.

"One of the largest logging companies was the B&C. A man by the name of John Porter was known as king of the logging crews. John was six-foot-four, blond-haired, blue-eyed, and had muscle on muscle. He was usually in a good mood, was never sick, and was never heard complaining or grumbling about anything. I suppose you would have to admit that he was a fair man and the other men often went to him to settle their disputes.

"I guess it was because of all these 'obvious flaws' that John was not what you could call a well-liked man. In fact, the men were darn right uncomfortable around him. It seemed unnatural to them to be such a goody-two-shoes all the time, not to mention that he was a total bore. Let me tell you, when a man cuts himself shaving he's supposed to cuss. When he eats so much his seams are going to bust and his stomach finally belches, he's not supposed to cover his mouth sheepishly and make apologies. Instead, a man should grin with satisfaction, and nod his head proudly at his accomplishment," Uncle said.

"What made things worse for the men was the fact that John could outwork each and every one of them. Nobody could match him, whether spike-climbing a tall tree to top it, using an axe, or wrestling a tree into place to harness. John was the biggest, strongest, and perhaps the best looking man around. That fact alone made him completely intolerable to others.

"Every other Sunday a traveling priest named

Father Nathan Able would come to the main camp to preach about man's sins and temptations. There was always a great turnout. You see, curiosity always got the best of the men. No one wanted to take the chance that there was something out there he hadn't yet done—something he might miss out on.

"Of course, what everyone looked forward to the most on those Sundays was the company of Miss Emily Corning, the daughter of the half-owner of the B&C Logging Company. The Cornings lived along King's Row on Lake George, but she and her father often stayed at the Sportsmen Hotel in North Creek. Their visits always corresponded with the church services. After services, Mr. Corning got a progress report, followed by a short tour.

"Emily was a looker. She had long dark hair, an angel face, and a figure that made men mumble. I will admit, being twenty miles back in the woods and her being the only woman a guy would see for months at a time could affect one's faculties. But I'm telling the story and I say she was one 'hot tamale.' "

Uncle had gone too long without stopping for air. He had to rest to regain his breath. While Uncle gasped, Jed jumped up and grabbed a couple of long necks from the bar. Nesy added a few more logs to the fire and both were back in their seats before Uncle could resume. Uncle took the time to give them a frown, followed by a snarl, before he started again.

"Where was I, oh yeah. . . ," he said. "It was well known throughout the camp that John Porter considered Emily his gal. Men there gave a lot of thought to the ways of women. You could often hear these philosophers in camp sharing tales of a past encounter, or a hopeful tryst they planned for the future. The outcome always depended on correctly interpreting the signals a girl gives out during conversations. It was agreed that the way of women required a great deal of study.

"No one could quite figure out how John Porter had gotten the signal from Emily. Oh, she was always polite to him, but it never seemed to amount to much as far as the men could see. Some of the men thought John had gotten his signals crossed. But, from past experience, they knew to stay clear of her.

"If anyone spent too much time with her, or grinned a little too long while they were thinking whatever they were thinking, they found themselves on John's own crew. They usually ended up as John's work partner. He never had a cross word for them, nor threatened them with any act of violence. He didn't have to. The real torture was John's work pace. Many a man that got stuck working with John went to bed early smelling of Doc Turner's homemade joint and muscle cure-all. They'd be so stiff the next day that they couldn't even get out of bed, let alone walk—which meant the loss of a couple days pay.

"It was on the second Sunday in March. I believe the year was 1938. Mr. Corning and Emily were on their way to the main camp from the Sportsmen Hotel. There had been a little snow during the night, but it was an uncommonly warm day. Mr. Corning was cheerfully remarking that spring was going to be early this year. What he was really thinking was that the river would break free of ice soon and the winter timber harvest would get to the market early—meaning larger profits this year.

"When the Cornings came to the north country in winter, they rode the Red Rocket. The Rocket was a ten foot sleigh made of thick mahogany with a dark, reddish tint. The sleigh was pulled by two gentle giants, Fergus and Angus, both unusually large Clydesdales. On occasion Emily would drive, especially when her father was preoccupied—like now. Fergus and Angus usually knew where they were going and were not easily influenced, even by the person holding the reins.

"They were turning a sharp corner when, out of nowhere, a man appeared. The man had been standing with his back toward them, looking down the hillside at the gorge. The now frozen river had carved a deep path through the valley. He must have heard Fergus and Angus coming, yet he was in no apparent hurry to get out of the way. His eyes lingered on the arctic valley until the last possible second. When the horses were only a stride away, he turned sharply, held up his hands, and in a low voice said, 'Whoa.' It was as if someone had thrown over an anchor. Eight huge feet, or hooves I should say, locked into place. The team and sleigh slid forward and came to a halting stop that almost threw Emily and her father from the sleigh. When Mr. Corning and Emily regained their seats they were once again shocked, for Fergus and Angus were taking turns rubbing their heads against the man's chest while he vigorously rubbed behind their ears. Fergus and Angus had never shown any signs of affection, nor would anyone have expected any. With their elephant-like size and facial expressions that clearly said, 'Don't irritate us!' let's just say most people gave them a wide berth. So you can understand Emily and Mr. Corning's shock and loss of words.

"The stranger spoke first with a loud, 'Hello.' The man said that he had heard there was a logging company around that was doing some hiring.

"Mr. Corning, who was coming out of his shock now, answered, 'Yes, yes. I'm one of the owners, and we're on our way there now. Come aboard.'

"The man did so, taking the reins from Emily.

" 'My name's Pete,' he said, as he threw the reins over his shoulder. In the middle of shaking hands with Mr. Corning and smiling a nod to Emily, he looked up to Fergus and Angus. In a low, but clear voice, he said, 'Hey,' and they were off at a slow gallop. Fergus and Angus had never done anything before that you could call a gallop. The man who had introduced himself as Pete started to whistle a lively Irish tune, which did not seem to repeat or end for that matter, until they reached camp.

"Two weeks after Emily's chance meeting of Pete on the trail, she was embarrassed, even if it was only to herself, because she was excited about seeing him again. She wondered why she felt this way. He was not an exceptionally handsome man. He was tall, lean, bone-faced, had straight black hair, and cool-colored eyes. He hadn't even said much to her the day of their first meeting. Although it did seem strange that just before she and her father left him at camp, Pete came right up to her, took her by the hand, looked her in the eyes and said, 'Good-bye. It's been a pleasure and I look forward to the next time we meet.'

"He smiled and nodded to her father, thanking him for the opportunity, meaning the job.

"In just two weeks Pete had become the most popular man in camp. He always had a new joke or great story to tell. The men liked to hear him sing or whistle one of his merry tunes. Best of all was the way Pete measured up to John Porter. John had seen Pete's, 'Good-bye until the next time we meet,' to Emily. Pete was immediately assigned to John's work crew all week as John's own partner. To everyone's surprise, not only did Pete keep up day to day, but before dinner each evening Pete liked to go for a long walk. He said the evening air helped increase his appetite.

"Well, Sunday morning rolled around again. Services were just about to start. Emily had been stalling at the front of the tent.

" 'We should be getting inside. Services are about to start,' John Porter said to Emily and her father.

"No one had seen Pete. The men were a little disappointed. You see, they were kind of hoping things would get to the boiling point soon. Emily finally gave up and followed her father and John into the tent. Emily took the aisle seat. Father Nathan Able was sucking in a deep breath—it was going to be a fire and brimstone sermon—the men's expectations were high.

"Suddenly the door shut! Pete stood at the rear of the church, wearing a black coat, trousers, and a shoe string tie over a stark white shirt. All eyes were riveted on him as he strolled down the aisle. Emily made room and almost forced John to sit on Mr. Corning's lap. John Porter was madder than a spring beaver. All his time and patience with Emily was going down the drain. She obviously had eyes for Pete. John's thoughts were quick and decisive. He had to find a way to humiliate Pete. It would have to be something Emily could witness. It had to be something so embarrassing that she would refuse to be seen in public with him. Now if John could prove to everyone that Pete was nothing but a loudmouth coward, that would do it. The men themselves would turn on him and probably drive him out of the camp.

"The first thing that came to John's mind was to pick a fight with Pete. If he gave him a thorough thrashing, a couple of black eyes or a broken nose, he bet Pete wouldn't look so good to Emily. As he thought this he wore a wide grin, but he soon started to rub his chin. Pete was the first man to ever match him at work. No, a fight might not be the right way to go, John thought."

Uncle paused and looked at his two listeners.

"It wasn't like it is now. Now-a-days, if a fight breaks out in town or at a bar, there always seems to be a handful of men to break things up—usually before anything good gets going. But back then, a fight was an event. Folks dropped everything to watch. More than likely there would be a lot of betting going on. In fact, people were known to get downright testy if someone were to quit a mite early in the fight. Now-a-days there are twenty-four hour medical facilities but back then it was mostly left up to God: body heal thyself."

Uncle got back to his story.

"Right in the middle of Father Nathan Able's 'Hell is Eternal,' there was an earth-shattering, thunder-like crack. Heads turned and stared at the wooden cross that hung above Father Nathan. Some of the men were hoping this was not some kind of personal message. Soon the air was filled with loud cracks. Men were hooting and hollering as they ran from the tent to the overview of the river, anticipating that the ice was going out.

" 'She's breaking loose!' someone hollered, meaning the whole river. John Porter remained seated throughout this once a year event. He continued grinning.

"It took a long month of hard work to do it. The holding pens that they had labored on so hard all winter—positioning the logs for release—were now empty. It would take another month to clean the river of strewn logs that had gotten hung up on one thing or another. Until now, there had been only two big log jams. But a little dynamite and the usual log-walking acrobatic skills that loggers used to manipulate the timber down the river, got everything moving smoothly. Everyone was too busy to give much thought to the rivalry between John and Pete—everyone that is except John.

"After the Sunday morning services a week later, John made his move. The usual crowd piled up in front of the main tent, discussing who did and didn't have first-hand knowledge of the day's sermon.

"Pete stood in front of Mr. Corning and Emily saying, 'If they stack the logs in the holding pens a little differently it would increase their holding capacity.'

"Emily stared at him intently, but I'm not sure if she was listening," Uncle added.

"John strolled right up to Pete and gave him a two-handed shove, landing Pete right on his butt.

" 'You must think Mr. Corning and the rest of

us are fools,' John bellowed. 'You may be able to beguile Emily, since she hasn't much experience at the ways of men like you, but don't kid yourself. We all know what you're up to and I'm not going to stand for it any longer.'

"Pete was getting up and moving in fast, in a fighting stance, when he heard, 'I challenge you to a river race. The winner stays and the loser leaves camp—right then and there.'

"John laid out the whole contest in front of everyone.

" 'We start right now at the big pool at Blue Ledges. The race ends where Thirteenth Lake Stream enters the Hudson. There is just one rule: once you set foot in or on the river the contest starts. If you leave the shoreline of the river for any reason you automatically forfeit.'

"John stomped off in the direction of the Blue Ledges. There was nothing Pete could do but follow.

"Pete was right in the middle of the crowd that had gathered at the pool at Blue Ledges. The Blue Ledges is a large, slow-moving pool where the water makes a deep bend. The south shore has a one hundred twenty-foot, slate-like embankment, straight up. There was a great deal of confusion as men were giving and taking odds, making bets.

John came out of nowhere running full-steam through the crowd, tackling Pete into the river and giving him a terrific head-butt in the process. When Pete got to his feet, he was chest deep in the river. There was a knot on his forehead large enough to cast a shadow and a trickle of blood coming from it. John was dragging himself onto a long log.

"Once he was standing on top of the log, he started rolling it slowly, working one end and then the other. John was known to be one of the best log-walkers on the river. Pete started to cuss, because John was wearing river spikes. In all the commotion Pete hadn't thought everything through.

"John began screaming, 'Remember, now that you're in the river the contest has begun. If you get out, you lose.'

"In the old days, if you got hustled or, as we used to say, 'you grabbed hold of the short end of the stick,' it was nobody's fault but your own. The philosophy was what the city lawyers call 'buyers best beware' clause," Uncle said.

"The last thing Pete heard was someone complaining, 'It's not fair. This doesn't count ...oh, that stinker John.'

"When Pete started swimming over to a log that had been forced on top of a rock, a cheer went up from the crowd. It was only a six-foot log and it came loose easily. Some of the spectators shouted, 'It's too small,' meaning that the log wasn't big enough to support a man standing on top of it. They were even further baffled when Pete snatched up a piece of driftwood that wasn't much bigger than an axe handle.

"One man in the crowd shouted, 'First you got to catch him before you can beat him with a club.'

"The crowd roared with laughter.

"Just before the laughter died down, Old Gus, a senior logger by anyone's standard, shouted, 'I'd bet a week's wages on Pete.'

" 'You're crazy but I'll take your money,' someone replied.

"It wasn't long before some of the men were scratching their heads while others were cursing Pete with respect-like praise. Pete climbed on one end of the log and was straddling it like a horse. Using his stick as a paddle, Pete handily navigated the first stretch of rapids now known as Mile Long Rapids.

"They were alternately shouting cheers of encouragement and ridicule about Pete's new yacht as they ran along the shoreline.

" 'You can't say he's not game enough,' Old Gus shouted.

"Emily and her father were standing nearby.

"Another one yelled, 'John's got a pretty good head start. He's almost through the strain. Pete will never make it through like that.'

"The strain is a narrow series of funnels. The river is unwillingly forced through the narrow openings, causing it to churn violently. The result is several very nasty waves called hydros—the kind that suck you under and keep you there. A logger will usually jump from his log to a large outcropping of rocks. The rocks indicate the start of the strain. With a little climbing and some simple footwork from rock to rock, one could meet the log at the end of the strain like John had.

"Pete was rowing hard trying to enter the strain on the right-hand side of the river in hopes that he would not hit the hydros head-on. The last thing anyone saw was Pete wrapping a huge bear hug around his boat-like tree. The spectators raced around the bend to the churning holding pool where the strain emptied.

"There was no sign of Pete. The crowd grew quiet. Emily tugged on her father's arm in frustration. Old Gus shook his head saying, 'I guess that's the end of it then.'

"Folks were taking one last look at the pool as if in agreement with Gus, when Pete, still wrapped around his log, spewed out of the churning waters into the air. It looked just like a war movie, when the submarine emerges from the shadowy depths. The log, with Pete still attached, cleared some air time coming down with a loud crack! It happened so close to the shoreline that several people from the crowd were hit by the spray.

"The next stretch of river is comparatively calm, with only five to six foot waves to contend with. The spectators could no longer easily follow the shoreline nor keep up with the pace of the river. Horse-drawn carts were fetched and in them the crowd raced to the finish line.

"There is a spot where a large boulder towers out of the river, creating a slow moving eddy behind it—this is what you boys now call Elephant Rock. John decided to take a break. He was sitting there daydreaming about how he bested Pete; it would be clear sailing with Emily. As he was staring off in his daydream haze a voice suddenly broke in.

" 'It is a fine day isn't it?' Pete had just ridden his little boat right by him.

"The last obstacle was, of course, what the raft guides have labeled so well, the Black Hole. The Black Hole is made by some natural irregular formations of rock ledges at the bottom of the river.

During high waters, going into the Black Hole is just like tripping and falling down a deep well.

"Pete and John were neck and neck just before entering the 'Hole.' John was just about to jump to the rocks along the shoreline when the back end of his log unexpectedly bumped Pete's. John was thrown head first into the river.

"Gus was the first one to see them approaching the finish line. He tried to holler but he was choking so hard on his chaw of tobacco that he could only point. There were shouts of . . . let's call it exasperation, from the crowd.

"Pete and John crossed the finish line wrapped around Pete's little lifeboat log. They were both kicking their feet, laughing, and singing the first verse of 'My Wild Irish Rose.' They looked like a couple of drowned river rats.

"Gus was finally able to expectorate his chew. He proceeded to cuss and stomp his feet up and down the shoreline.

" 'Things sure aren't like they used to be. You used to be able to count on people to carry on a good feud, fight to the death and all, but not anymore. You younger generations are nothing more than soft, melon-headed wimps,' Gus burst out.

Having listened to the story intently, Nesy spoke up.

"You've got to be kidding me, Uncle. Are you going to tell me they became best friends? What about the girl, Emily?"

"Well," Uncle replied, "that's the kicker. Her father, Mr. Corning, just about busted his gut telling Gus.

"When Pete and John got out of sight at the flats after the strain, Mr. Corning and Emily hopped into the Red Rocket. Gus thought they were headed to the finish line with the rest of the crowd, when Mr. Corning called Gus over.

" 'Gus, make sure you tell John and Pete I'm sorry we couldn't stay for the finish. But, I want to hear all the details on my next visit. Emily and I are getting a late start as it is, and we have to be in Glens Falls tomorrow morning. Emily is catching the noon train for Boston. She's off to Miss Whitney's finishing school for young ladies,' Mr. Corning said. 'I'm sure going to miss her.'

"Gus and Mr. Corning shared a quiet laugh, when Gus commented, 'I don't reckon you'll be alone in that department.' "

Uncle was staring into the fireplace almost dozing off as Jed and Nesy left the room. At the doorway on their way out, Jed turned and quietly said, "Good night, Uncle Pete, good night."

THE FLY, THE FISH, AND THE FOOLISH

It was summer. Spring had come and gone. Nesy had become a recognized and welcomed face in town. This meant that the locals would engage him in small talk: need rain; muggy day; Bill Robinson's daughter is showing again; Rick Parker lost another front tooth Saturday night.

Everyone knew the town headlines. Outsiders might find this verbal "newspaper" obsolete. But in Tavern's Corner, life's pace is a little slower and the real fun with the news was the enhancement of the facts. Every time a "headline" was retold, someone got a chance to make it a little more interesting. When the Robinson's built a new outhouse in the back of the barn, it was called the new wing. It was said that the Sheraton was secretly funding the project. When the tavern added rice to the menu, it was said that Ma, a seventy-year-old woman, was secretly seeing a retired Chinese sailor. If questioned, she merely grinned and gave an abrupt grunt. Ironically, soon after she heard the rumor, soy sauce was found next to the ketchup and mustard. It's said that life is what you make of it. Out here it's also what you can get someone else to believe.

Nesy had been coming up to the Adirondacks just about every other weekend. He usually stayed in one of the spare cabins in back of the Tavern House. Coincidentally, these trips corresponded with his wife's trips to her mother's. She did not mind his double life; in fact she saw a change in him—a confident assertiveness that hadn't been there before. Nesy was always a very kind man without a temper. He had a boyish innocence when it came to women. That's what had attracted her to him to begin with, but now, she was very happy with the new Nesy.

Nesy was listening to the town news one morning during breakfast in the tavern room. The conversation drifted, as it usually did, to fishing. In the middle of someone's fish story, Nesy blurted out, "I always meant to learn how to fish." There was a pause in the conversation. The only thing that could be heard was Ma in the kitchen clearing her throat.

Jed suddenly broke out in laughter as everyone else exchanged looks.

"There's that city sarcasm boys," Jed quickly said. "Why, after the stories he's told me and the pictures I've seen, I'll bet he could pull a Marlin out of a pickle bucket on a hand line with a wine cork for a bobber and a safety pin for a hook. He's one of the best fishermen to ever hit the hills."

One or two of the boys rubbed their chins, but if Jed said so, they were willing to go along.

Jed abruptly left the room and returned promptly carrying a bundle of poles and gear. "Come on, Nesy, I've been waiting for the proper time to trap you into showing me some of those fishing tricks of yours."

That morning Jed briefly introduced Nesy to bait fishing; worms. He said it was important to have a base and to learn an appreciation of the way of things. In the afternoon, Nesy learned the use of lures, spinners, and spoons. Jed talked about feeding habits and water currents. They changed locations many times, from slow pocket water to rushing rapids. They fished well into the night, going from plug fishing to an anchored double snare rig for bullheads.

It was midnight when Jed dropped Nesy off at the cabin. "Get a good night sleep. I'll wake you at six. You just finished a basic introduction to fishing. Tomorrow, I'm going to tell you the story of the fly and the fish."

To Jed, fly-fishing was a way of life. A philosophy, if you will. He'd say you had to understand and think like a fish—not only when and what he will eat, but where and how he likes it, what he will do when he's hooked, how far he will run, and to where. You don't reel in a fish on a fine tapered leader. You have to outthink him, exhaust him. You have to know when to let him run and when to bring him back. Fly-fishing is a chess game, with moves and counter moves. A trout doesn't exist on luck, he goes to school. He's constantly learning to adapt in order to survive. He has a hard life and one certainly has to admire his tenacity.

Nesy wondered just what Jed meant when he said there are some that are meant for the frying pan and others never meant to be caught. Nesy was starting to think that there was more to fishing, and perhaps to Jed, than he had first thought.

Once Nesy got the basics down, he soon became

an accomplished fisherman; Nesy and Jed's exploits soon became the common talk of the town. People would gather in the family room of the Tavern to hear all about their latest exploit, or fish stories as we might call them. In a small town it's just as important to tell a good fish story as it is to fish—you have to learn to dangle your bait.

On this particular Sunday, there was a larger crowd than usual at the Tavern. Beyond the regulars, there were several families and a couple of strays sitting around. Everyone was waiting eagerly to hear last week's story retold by the characters themselves.

The story took place at High Gorge at the Ausable River. It's a strange river, erratic and constantly changing. It can be calm and peaceful in one spot and bubbling to a boil in another just inches away. Within one step it can go from several inches to forty feet deep with twists and turns and enough force to tear a tree from it's roots, let alone knock a man down for a careless step.

The so-called entrance to the gorge starts at a thirty-five-foot cliff. Jed led the way. As they climbed over an edge, Nesy pointed out a roundish rock above them that was the size of a three-story house. It sat on a downward slant and he swore he saw it wiggle. Jed told him not to worry, that if old

Atlas should start to roll again . . . Nesy quickly interrupted, "What do you mean roll again?"

"Well, that rock got restless a long time ago and decided to shake loose from that mountain top," Jed explained. "Every once in a great while it takes a step or two. Uncle says it won't be happy till it gets to the river and joins some old friends." Nesy looked up at the cliff's ledge. They were about half way down. Great.

The gorge measured only twenty yards across, with a steep wall on one side. The river had a bend in it and the water was moving fast. A little ways downstream a large uprooted tree had tried unsuccessfully to block the river. Most of the water passed underneath, the rest slammed up against it sending a volcanic spray into the air. On the other side of the tree a small waterfall funneled into a large pool.

"There are two ways to fish this," Jed explained. "One is by doing a short roll cast from shore. By mending your line, you can get your fly to the other bank. Once your line hits the bend on a dead drift, you'll always find a school of hungry young trout there trying to stay out of the current. The other way is not so simple. You have to get out to the island and, by throwing your line up river into the bend, your fly will drift into that big eddy in the middle of the rapids. That's where the monsters lie."

"What island?" Nesy asked.

"It's out there just about an inch or two under the water," Jed replied. "You can't see the island until you are just about on top of it. You can get to it by jumping from rock to rock."

Nesy stared out into the rushing river as Jed stretched his jaw and wrinkled his forehead—Nesy suggested trying the island first. Uncle had said that Nesy was the kind that might surprise you. "There's more under the surface than you might believe."

Jed had turned his back as Nesy waded out to the first rock. Nesy knew Jed, he was pretending to play with his rigging. Any other time he would have his pole lined, fly tied, and be in the water in seconds.

The first jump was easy, if you can call it a jump. It was more of an exaggerated stretch of the legs, but adding three foot chopping waves really put the pressure on. He came up short on the second jump and ended up bear hugging a rock, having to drag himself to an upright position.

Standing and shaking the excess water off like a dog, he could see the so-called island. It was about four feet wide and two feet long. The water plowed into the rock forming a V-shape around it. The film from the spray was the only thing keeping the rock submerged. Nesy was just about done judging the distance and finishing an "Our Father" when his foot slipped from its place, forcing his body forward. A series of violent thrusts of arms and legs in various directions followed. The next thing he knew, he was standing on top of the island, not knowing how he got there but feeling a sense of achievement.

On his second cast, his fly, the one Uncle had tied for him the night before (calling it an apple dumpling), bounced off the rock wall on the other side right into a perfect dead drift. Nesy was thinking this quite an accomplishment, when out of nowhere a huge trout rose from the water and completely engulfed the fly. Instantly, the line zipped out of his reel. Just as Nesy recovered from the shock, the monster broke the water surface again with twisting acrobatics. It was all happening so fast. He heard Jed yelling from shore, "Make him earn it." Nesy looked at his reel; the fish was still taking out line, using the current to help him. Wetting his hand, he lightly pressed his forefingers against the reel spool, which slowed the fish down. It was plain to see the fish's plan. It was starting its dive and soon would be under the fallen tree.

When the fish reached the other side, it would break surface again and use the fallen tree to apply tension to the line, breaking it.

Nesy turned and looked at Jed. Jed just nodded his head and shrugged his shoulders at the inevitable outcome. Nesy frowned, looked down at his reel spool, pulled a large loop of line from it, and jumped into the river. He popped up once in front of the tree, grabbing a quick breath while trying to keep his pole behind him.

Jed scrambled along the shoreline to get to the pool. When he finally spotted Nesy, he was kneeling and holding one of the largest fresh water Browns ever seen in the Adirondacks. Nesy cradled the fish in his arms like a small child. He slowly bent over and loosened his grip, releasing the fish back into the river.

Nesy stood up when Jed approached, still knee deep in the river, and splashed a handful of water on his face. "I guess that was pretty stupid risking life, limb, and a bump on the head, and on top of it all, I lost the fish," Nesy said.

"Yeah, it looked like Old Marble Eye to me. Was one eye glossed over and did its lip look like it had been torn, leaving a whitish scar patch?"

Nesy lost all pretense. "That was him all right. It was a pain trying to remove the hook without hurting him. I hope he recovers okay."

Jed grinned, "Marble Eye, he'll be just fine and waiting patiently to test the next fool of a fisherman to come along." That brought some knowing smiles to the "regulars" at the Tavern that Sunday.

McQUIREN'S BOARDING HOUSE

Nesy took a swallow that shifted his Adam's apple. The roar of the river was growing louder, yet no ripples other than those made by their paddles showed.

Jed told Nesy to relax, "Remember, nice even strokes."

Nesy grunted a yes along with a couple of indistinguishable words. Unconsciously, his hands tightened around his paddle and he heard Jed say, "Get ready. Just around the corner the fun starts. Don't forget to lock your knees and don't sweat it. Remember, I've done this before."

"Yeah, but not with the Nesy factor," Nesy remarked. Jed rubbed his chin and commented that he hadn't really considered that.

What Jed didn't tell Nesy was that this week's rain had brought the river to a higher level than he had ever seen run in an open canoe before. He had two choices, put to shore or go on, which definitely meant taking the risk of a thorough thrashing from the river. Jed considered it. Both were wearing high float life jackets and old hockey helmets, which showed the scars of previous outings. Jed cleared his throat and mind at the same time. He had a good reason for going on. It was not for thrills or pride's sake, but he had to admit that this day's outing would make great telling Sunday at the Tavern House.

One week ago Nesy, Jed, and Uncle were sitting on the front porch of the Tavern House watching the sun set. Nesy remarked that he and his wife were ready to start a family. In fact, they were looking for someplace local as a second home. The area had something important that you couldn't quite nail down in words, but would be needed in the upbringing of kids.

"Want to be part of the community, huh?" Uncle replied.

The low hum of a generator coming from the

McQuiren's place broke the silence. McQuiren's Boarding House sits on the hill just at the edge of the so-called town. It depended on who you talked to as to what and where the "community" was. Some say, "there is no official title or name, no mayor, no police, and we have no good reason to want to be considered town folk." Others claim that it's embarrassing when asked where they are from to reply, "the Northern Hills of New York." It seems to come up short. The reply most would give is Tavern's Corner. This name doesn't quite make sense either. There is a tavern, which is definitely the center of town, but there are no corners, stop signs, or intersections. In fact, few would even hesitate when passing Tavern House.

Uncle's line of thought could sometimes be very hard to follow. His next statement was, "Next week the stray caterpillars will start to be found and next weekend would be perfect timing to hit the Blue Ledges for Browns."

Uncle had a way about him that made the simplest of things seem so important. "Ms. McQuiren added one more mouth to the table last week by taking in Dave Robinson's boy while Dave's off looking for work."

The McQuiren's place was an unofficial boarding house. It's hard to tell how it started but Ms.

McQuiren was known to have anywhere from seven to seventeen temporarily homeless children. I say homeless, not faceless. There weren't enough faces around to not recognize one.

There's a certain closeness in Tavern's Corner that's a rarity these days. It's probably because, try as you might, no one can remain a stranger. As far as the McQuiren's kids go, the names might not always be remembered, but their faces are. There was the blond haired boy who always stole fresh candy apples that he found on Ma's counter on Sunday afternoons. Toad was the red-headed freckle-faced girl. The town had already started a small college fund for her. Even at her age it was evident that she was going to be a wiz. There was the stubborn boy known as "Root," already a natural leader. Someday others would rely on him for his sound judgment. In Tavern's Corner, no one would aspire or normally wish it upon anyone to become a politician. It was considered something that happened to the less fortunate. The exception to that though would be Root, who was tailor-made for this profession and the country was in desperate need for some old fashion common sense.

It was the way of things that one didn't ask for help or expect it. Some while back Ma donated her old chest freezer to Ms. McQuiren, which held enough to feed a large army under siege for a full year. It took Dave Coker's John Deere to haul it there. Jed and the boys took it upon themselves to keep it stocked with fish and venison. There were rumors about Jed and Ms. McQuiren, but Jed being Jed, not much was ever said aloud. Once a year, when Uncle gave the word, Jed would take to the hills to catch as many trout as he could. In the evenings, one might hear a rifle shot echoing through the mountaintops. In three days Jed would have the old freezer filled with trout and venison.

There was only one problem, Erin Prod. Erin was Jed's childhood rival. They had managed to keep it going all these years, more out of tradition than real animosity. He was the wannabe local FBI agent but, in reality, was a part time forest ranger. He was the only official anything for miles around. Over the last couple of years it seemed he was getting a little uppity. People noticed that he had sewn official looking patches on all his shirts and from time to time he would be seen studying old wanted posters he'd get from the Post Office in Keeneville.

It all started a few years ago when a state trooper stopped to ask him directions while escorting a young kid back to his parents. It seemed he had borrowed his parents' car for a short joy ride.

In a week's time, Erin had told the story all over town of how he had helped the police with their prisoner and aided his transportation back to the proper authorities. He had retold the story so many times and liked his imaginary role so much that he actually believed it. He was now stuck trying to live up to his own conceptions. Fortunately, he was aided by his inflated ego.

Last Sunday, Erin Prod was sitting in the Tavern House drinking black coffee and flipping through his wanted posters when he heard someone snicker. Enraged, he looked around the room for someone to put in their place, thinking that would get him respect from the others. Before he could come to his senses, he told Jed that he was one of the worst hoodlums in the area and that he wasn't going to tolerate it anymore. If he tried to pull any shenanigans this year to fill McQuiren's freezer, he would see to it that he was arrested. Jed never replied. Erin knew he had gone too far and Jed was not one to be pushed. Jed merely smiled a wide grin, which was more than enough to completely take the steam out of Erin, who was thinking that the nearest dentist was a two-hour drive.

Uncle walked nonchalantly between them, looking down at his pipe as if something was wrong with it.

"Now Erin, that's awfully big talk from someone who has to take a compass reading to get to and from the outhouse. You best get now and we'll forget about the fool you've made of yourself today."

That was like a slap in the face. After that, Erin Prod was bound and determined to catch Jed and everyone knew it. Uncle said things were getting a little dull and a little pot stirring was good for the community.

The quickest, and some might say the easiest, way to get a canoe to the Blue Ledges on the upper Hudson River is to shoot the rapids of the Indian River, which spills right into the Hudson. The long and short of Jed and Nesy's trip was the two hundred yards before the Indian meets the Hudson at a place known as Guides Hole. Here the canoe got caught in a large hydrowave, a circular wave going in the opposite direction of the river.

Jed was sucked out of the boat and just before the canoe was beyond what would be considered floating, Nesy remarked, "I'm glad all I have to do is paddle. I can't begin to see how you're picking your path through this mess of waves and rocks." The three of them, Nesy, Jed, and the upside down canoe, floated into a big pool at Blue Ledges. Luckily, what gear they brought was still tied into the boat.

After an hour of cursing, coughing, and laughing, they were dried out and Jed explained about snare line fishing. There is no sport or romance to it. It's somewhat unethical and illegal, but also the quickest and easiest way to catch a lot of fish in a short period of time.

Four hours later, Jed and Nesy were back in the canoe. They had snared over forty browns. The rest of the Hudson River was fairly tame, but there were one or two exciting moments. One landed Nesy in the back of the canoe alongside Jed, who commented, "I think it would be best if we didn't switch places this time around."

Two hundred yards before the boat launch, Jed tugged at his pack trying to get something out. At first Nesy had no idea what it was, but when he realized it was a child's inflatable toy, he thought Jed had lost his marbles. Jed's face turned blue inflating a large duck that a child wears around his waist to keep him afloat.

"Unless I miss my guess, we'll see company at the boat launch," Jed said. As he lowered the duck into the water, he asked Nesy to do him a favor.

"When we get close to shore, I want you to stand and wave."

Sure enough, Erin Prod was there with one of his little buddies, both wearing their official green uniforms. Nesy stood to wave. Jed immediately hollered, "Sit down," while at the same time cut the rope that went to the inflated duck. He then rocked the boat, which sent Nesy into a professional balancing act comparable to the best of the high wire acts. Jed hated doing it, but just as Nesy looked like he would recover, Jed flipped the canoe.

Erin Prod shouted at them from shore as Nesy and Jed splashed water back and forth like angry children, each blaming the other for the clumsiness that tipped the canoe.

Erin was hollering, "You won't find it so funny when I site you both for illegal fishing. I hope you have a lot of fish 'cause I'm going to cite you separately for each one. It's going to cost you a fortune. You'll both probably lose your licenses and maybe then some people around here will know that I mean business."

"Well that's all well and good," replied Jed, "but who said we've been fishing? You're welcome to look through everything once we get to shore. But I'll tell you, you won't find any fish." At that, Jed looked over his shoulder at the inflated duck which was well on its way downstream.

All eyes were on it. Erin hollered, but in his frustration all that came out was, "Why you." Turning to his comrade he yelled, "Come on, we have to catch that duck before one of his brothers gets to it." They jumped into the car and spent the day chasing the duck down the river.

Nesy and Jed put the boat to their shoulders and as they walked out of the river, water drained out of the boat and from their clothes. Nesy turned and noticed that Jed's pants were still bulging at the seams.

"Will ya hurry it up? Let's get this canoe in the back of the truck. I've got twenty fish down each pant leg and its starting to tickle."

Late the next day, Erin parked his car in front of the Tavern House and sat listening. He knew Jed would be lining up the cross hairs on his rifle at just about dusk. If he was lucky, he might be able to catch Jed red-handed. Just then Uncle walked onto the porch and sat in his rocker. At exactly the moment the sun ducked behind Macomb Mountain—8:30 p.m.—there were gun shots everywhere. In backyards, hillsides, and mountaintops it seemed as if a small war had broken out.

"It's not over!" Erin shouted at the top of his lungs.

The next morning, Erin, followed by a state trooper, pulled up to McQuiren's Boarding House. Erin informed Trooper Moore, "The freezer is in the back of the house." As they walked up to the porch,

Trooper Moore noticed all the old toys scattered about. A couple of toddlers took turns on a peppermint stick. What he guessed to be a twelve-year-old boy was splitting wood in the side yard, and having a stubborn time with a thick piece. At Trooper Moore's feet sat a little, red-headed, freckle-faced girl who was playing with a frog.

The trooper bent over and effortlessly picked up the little girl, keeping her at arm's length. They stared at each other for a minute and then exchanged ear to ear smiles. Trooper Moore turned towards Erin, who had been doing some looking around of his own, and handed him the little girl.

"Don't waste my time again."

Erin was left standing on the steps with the little girl still in his arms. The girl made a deep sigh, for the frog had jumped from her hands and left a damp mess behind. Despite the children's stares, Erin Prod laughed a good, long, loud laugh.

THE YANKEES FAN
AND A NUMBER SIX FLY

Now, a well experienced fisherman like Nesy knows all of the excuses. It's too hot, too sunny, too windy, too late in the morning, and too early in the afternoon. Of course, the most common excuse is: "I don't have exactly the right fly with me."

With three or four fly boxes, and over 300 flies, it's amazing how often that can happen. It's also true, the longer a fisherman goes without catching a fish, the faster he changes from fly to fly. It's a panic thing, searching for one magical fly that is mixed in with all those other losers in your box.

Since the release of old Marble Eye, Nesy had become a very enthusiastic fisherman. He didn't like the idea of returning home skunked. Nesy was thinking what pitch to try to throw by Nancy. He needed to return home with at least a good fish story. For his sake, she usually took a swing at high and outside.

Nesy noticed a young boy scrambling down the embankment that he previously had descended, Pete Rose-style, face first. The boy was wearing an old pair of Chuck Taylor all-star sneakers, tattered jeans, and a plain white T-shirt topped off with a traditional Yankee's baseball cap. He stood there with a long, hand-me-down bamboo fly rod in one hand and a container the size of a wristwatch box in the other.

The boy stared at Nesy for some time. His mouth hung wide open like church doors on a Sunday morning. Nesy figured the combination of surprise at running into another fisherman and envious delight over Nesy's new rig caused the boy to gawk.

Nesy was waist high in the Ausable River, just outside of Wilmington in Essex County. He looked like a pro. He was wearing a big straw hat with a black sash around that said "Nike" and a red checkered shirt with a gray Orvis vest with wide, inflatable shoulder straps. His waders were the newest L.L. Bean; double knee, lightweight, breathable-type with built-in gravel guard cuffs. He was using a Powell nine-foot rod with a white ivory reel seat that held a custom Able reel. At the time, he was throwing 70 yards of phosphorescent yellow line. My, my he thought, I must be quite a sight.

Nesy gave the boy a head nod and waited. It's always a tense couple of moments when two fishermen meet riverside. Traditionally there is the, "Any luck?" question, followed by "Have you tried this or that?" Any knowledgeable fisherman responds with a loud and clear, "Some." That response to another knowledgeable fisherman means he knows something. It is a good chess match. Each strategist is maneuvering to gain key info, which may instantly pay off by landing a lunker on your very next cast.

The boy pointed upstream with a questioning nod of his head. Nesy nodded back, meaning go ahead. Nesy was feeling a little cheated. He told himself the boy was obviously an inexperienced player, or perhaps he felt a little over-matched and that's why he skirted playing the verbal game.

Nesy was doing him no real favor. The pool ahead looked big and deep. He figured the only way to fish it would be from shore, doing a big roll cast. The thick brush along the bank would make it no picnic.

Nesy was just starting to feel a little sorry for the kid when he watched him leap from a boulder feet first into the river. Holding his pole and fly box in one hand above the water, and doing an Australian crawl with the other, he made his way to the center of the pool. The young Yankees fan looked like he was treading water for a moment or so, and then he broke out with a wide grin. The next thing Nesy saw, the boy was less than knee deep in the water, obviously standing on some sort of huge underwater rock ledge.

He opened his little cardboard fly box and itched his head under his cap. Nesy smiled to himself; poor kid, I should give him a couple of flies and maybe a quick lesson on casting before I leave.

The boy tied on his fly without much fuss and threw about 20 feet of line across the current. With his left hand he pulled about an eight-foot loop of line from his reel. With an effortless, upstream, line-mending, loop-feeding maneuver, the line slid through the pole guides. "This kid isn't so bad," Nesy said to himself.

All of a sudden his pole arced, the rod tip almost touching the water. The Yankees fan held his pole high, trying to keep it pointed toward the sky. His line was singing as it zipped from his reel.

Nesy maneuvered closer to watch the show when the boy's fish broke the surface. Nesy stumbled, falling into the water on all fours. It was a struggle, but he never broke eye contact, as if somehow, if he had, the fish would be lost. "Oh sweetness!" Nesy hollered as he scrambled to shore. The boy remained in expressionless concentration.

For the next 20 minutes, Nesy watched a real artist at work. The fish ran downstream using the power of the current to distance himself from his adversary. The young Yankees fan did not fight the run. Instead, he gave the fish all of the line he wanted. The boy scooped a hat full of water and poured some over his reel and doused himself with the rest as he placed his hat firmly back on his head. The unmistakable, high-pitched hum of the reel changed tone slightly. The fish jumped from the river three, maybe four times, as if it could already feel the heat of the frying pan. Each time the fish leapt, it thrashed its head back and forth while arching its back. It reminded Nesy of a crazed horse at a rodeo trying to throw some cowboy from his back.

The fish was a smart one, but the kid was no rookie. Each time the fish tried to free itself from the hook, the boy instinctively lowered the tip of his pole to release the line tension. Every time the fish resisted, the boy reeled a little line back.

It was a big, really big, fish. As the boy drew the fish closer, Nesy could see the bright colors of an Adirondack rainbow trout. The show was just about over, or so Nesy thought. The fish was about three inches under the water line, coming along nicely. Nesy could see the gills flaring. Suddenly, without warning, the fish sprang to life once again. With incredible speed it broke for shore.

The trout made for a fallen tree that dipped into the river. If it could reach the tree, it would only take a second for the fish to hang the line and escape. The boy didn't try to stop the run. Instead, he slowly moved the pole from his left shoulder to his right, extending his arm and pole as far outward as possible. This perfectly countered the rainbow's run. Before the fish realized what had happened, it was nine feet upstream of the tree.

The boy never touched the fish. The rainbow was arm's reach away, exhausted and slowly panting. The boy, with his bamboo pole tucked under his arm, seemed to be talking to the fish while he held the line with his hand. After a couple of minutes he snaked his hand down the line to the hook and held it firmly. After a time, the fish jerked his head and broke free.

When the boy came to shore Nesy remarked,

"That was quite a show." The boy looked up at him with a questioning face. To him it was just fishing. After some basic fish talk, Nesy found himself compelled to ask what kind of fly he'd been using. The boy looked up from the mangled specimen and replied: "A Number Six." If he was going to replace it, he said, he would have to go looking for Willie, the neighbor's cat.

The young Yankees fan opened his little cardboard box. Inside there were six cotton balls glued down, each numbered: one, two, and so forth. Each cotton ball held some kind of homemade fly. Number One was made with hair from his dog, Curly; Number Two from his mother's good red sweater. With any luck and some leftover tuna casserole, he would be able to replace that Number Six tonight.

The boy trotted off home, mumbling something about history homework. As far as the rest of Nesy's day fishing went—"High and outside, a swing and a miss."

THE BUYING OF THE OLD MILL HOUSE

Over a couple of longnecks one evening, Nesy announced that next weekend he would like to rent the corner master suite of the Tavern House. Uncle asked what the occasion was, stating he didn't mean to be nosy but Ma would need some persuading.

"You see, for the last four years or so Ma's had some sort of fantasy about Paul Newman getting stranded around here overnight. All I really know is that it's got something to do with the two of them, that king-sized goose down feather bed, and that gallon of rum-scented Jamaican cocoa-butter oil she keeps next to her bed that gets hot when its rubbed against the skin," Uncle said.

The visual imagery sent a case of the willies to all throughout the tavern. Jed, Luke, Earl, Nesy, and a few of the other folks hanging out immediately filled the room with moans, groans, oohs, ahhs, and minor cursing, followed by large gulping swallows of beer. The final effort to rid themselves of the image, vigorous jerks of the head, looked as if they were shaking an Etch-A-Sketch toy, erasing the picture.

Nesy informed everyone that he would be bringing Mrs. Nesmond, Nancy, next weekend. All were to be on their best behavior. If everything went as planned, meaning if she gave the okay, he would make Uncle an offer on the Old Mill House out on Old Mill Creek.

"Makes good sense," Jed interrupted, "plenty of fishing holes nearby, and the old cottage has plenty of room for guests."

Earl turned to Luke and whispered, "I told ya, just about all city folks are millionaires. Imagine owning and living in two homes."

Well, everything did work out. In fact, folks were downright taken aback. Truth be told, there was a little wagering going on concerning the qualities of Mrs. Nesmond's appearance. A 1-to-10 scale was decided upon with Uncle elected as judge. Uncle was told the biggest contributing factors to grade Mrs. Nesmond: weight, growths of any kind, total body hair, and, last but not least, disposition.

To everyone's surprise, Nancy, Mrs. Nesmond, was quite a looker, fairly long brown hair, kickin' figure, and a pleasant smile. Most of all, she wasn't afraid to laugh out loud, whether taking or giving. She fit in very quickly. Sunday evening, when the town folk gathered on the front porch of the Tavern House to wave good-bye to Nesy and Nancy, she turned once more with a wave and that infectious smile, saying, "See you next time."

Earl leaned over to Luke, "I told you, he's got to be a millionaire."

Nesy did indeed buy the Mill House. On the way home Nesy commented to Nancy, "I hope you don't think I took advantage of Uncle at all. Perhaps Uncle was a little off balance with the whole deal. He did seem insistent on closing it though, and drawing up the contract on the spot."

Nancy hid her smile with her hand. "It did seem like Uncle had some last minute reservations, didn't it? What did he say was needed, sentimental compensation?" Nancy found it harder to suppress her laughter this time. A small smirk slipped out. She covered it with a cough.

Uncle had some last minute reservations for sentimental reasons, he had said when agreeing on the closing cost. "The Old Mill House used to have a garden in the backyard," he said with a sigh.

Next thing Nesy knew he was volunteering to hoe and seed a garden in the backyard of the Tavern House. The two old tree stumps needed to come out, of course, and a nearby white birch that was about to fall needed to come down. Before Nesy could stack the birch wood on the porch after splitting it, he would have to repair some floorboards. To get to the floorboards he'd have to move a few things to the barn. So things wouldn't get wet in the barn, some of the shingles would have to be replaced. Nesy didn't remember just how contact papering Ma's cupboards got on the list of things Uncle added to the back of the contract. Nor did he remember just how supplying Uncle with a freshwater rainbow trout once a week for the month of June came into the deal either.

Thank God they have indoor plumbing or I'd be digging Uncle a new outhouse, Nesy thought with relief. Nancy and Nesy's thoughts must have been along the same lines because they both started laughing at the same time.

"Well," Nancy said, "at least we get to keep our first born. Uncle wouldn't be able to get any work out of her for at least seven more months anyway. Jean is a nice name, don't you think?" Nancy commented.

Nesy's mouth was left hanging open like a barn door at milking time. Just a swingin' in the breeze.

A PATH LESS TROD—
AN EXTRAORDINARY HIKE

Jed was happy to realize that rising early some- how gets easier as one grows older. The apprecia- tion of a spankin' brand new day without the aid of a time clock, and the fact that we seldom seem to have reason to stay up past midnight help make it so.

Jed was not quite sure where his adventure was going to take him, after breakfast that is!

The Silver Star Diner in Chestertown, just off I-87 in Warren County, has always been a classic starting point. Jed was on his second cup of black stuff, awaiting his skillet of eggs, when the older couple at the corner table caught his attention.

He noted the way they interacted with each other. Without effort or strain they tended to, talked, and listened to one another. When their coffees arrived, the man took the utmost care in measuring the cream and sugar, shaking the excess sugar loose of the spoon before stirring it in and pushing the cup her way. She was busy comparing our current president's sexual activities to some of the past presidents while searching for a raspberry jelly amongst the endless grape and strawberry to spread on his wheat toast. The conversation moved around at a quick rate. From the garden, with this year's tomato and zucchini horde and where to unload the excess, to foreign trade policy, and the present worth of the dollar compared to just 50 years ago. They talked about the past as if it was yesterday. Trips they had been on and the years it took them to finally climb the 48, no 46 he corrected, highest peaks in the Adirondacks.

"Sarah," the old man said, "do you remember Macomb Mountain? Why don't we take a ride over there sometime? We'll take in Elk Lake and sneak a peek at that fancy lodge."

Sarah said that of the High Peaks, Macomb was

always her favorite. "It always seemed like we had the whole mountain just to ourselves." Macomb never got the same trampling as the other peaks, and the view from the summit looking out over Elk Lake was unmatched as far as she was concerned. When she recalled that lunch with the iced champagne, neither one had to speak as their thoughts could be seen in each other's faces.

Before he knew it, Jed somehow found himself seated at their table. His home fries needed ketchup—he was out—and he surely wanted to hear more about Macomb Mountain. Their conversation started with Jed mentioning, "Kennedy was a president you could at least respect." The older woman laughed while the gray-haired man quickly agreed.

———————

On his last outing Jed had hiked an old standard High Peak. The time before that it was Mount Marcy in Keene with a local kids' group. It had not been his first time. Don't get me wrong, Jed thought, the view from the peak is never disappointing. It's just, well it's a shame you have to share it with a herd of sheep. The trails are as crowded as the check out lines at the grocery store on Gobbler Day. It is so busy you have to make sure to stay on the right side of the trail as you ascend to stay out of the traffic that's descending. The view is outstandingly panoramic, but it's kind of like someone standing up in the middle of a movie in the row in front of you.

To Jed something is lost. This is not how the Adirondacks are meant to be seen. The Adirondacks are umpteen square miles and most of its visitors are all drawn to the same half dozen High Peaks. It's just common sense that they can't take the trampling they're getting year after year and Jed could see no reason, when some four thousand feet above sea level, to look out over anyone's shoulder.

Benny, Sarah's husband, had given Jed directions. Get back on 87, three exits to 29. Head west five to ten miles where there will be a sign for Elk Lake just after the buffalo herd. Jed remembered someone telling him about somebody starting a buffalo farm over that way, though he thought it was some sort of inside joke at his expense, but as his head rotated in awe at those giants grazing across the hillside, he knew better.

Leaving the parking lot, grabbing his day pack with the basics that every experienced woodsman always carries, Jed checked to make sure his journal was handy, for Benny had labored over drawing him a basic map and some notes for the hike.

As Jed reached the summit, he embraced the feeling that perhaps, just maybe, no one has stood in this exact spot before. Certainly not on an identical fall day as this one, with the endless blending of colors unfolding at your feet as far and wide as the eyes could see.

Jed couldn't help but think that people should follow the advice of those two people in love and check this out for themselves.

OLD BEN

At about 9 A.M., a family of four pulled their wagon into Tavern's Corner. They were looking for a hot spot to do a little skiing. An hour or two of Uncle's tall tales later they were on their way to Long Lake in Hamilton County. Uncle had assured them it was just the spot and told them to look up an old friend of his, Ben, if they got the chance.

Ben, meanwhile, rubbed a brick of wax against the backs of his wooden skis as small white clouds of smoke from his old pipe curled around his face. He lived alone these last five years on the north side of Long Lake. Ben considered his home to be the center of the Adirondack Mountains. He, his wife, and four children had spent the last thirty some-odd years building this camp. Progress had been a little slow as of late but his determination remained undaunted. His children, four beautiful girls, all grown with children of their own, continually tried to convince him to move closer to (not necessarily in) the Albany/Colonie area where they now resided.

His children may never understand, but his Adirondack home is so thickly intertwined with the days and memories of his life that he would be far lonelier if he were to ever leave it.

Ben could hear the car coming down Rock Bottom Lane. He stood up and nodded as it passed and as he did so his eyes fixed on the little curly haired girl sitting in the far back of the station wagon. In an arm hugging style usually reserved for a Teddy Bear, she cradled a jumbo bag of cheese popcorn. The other hand was busy adding more corn to her already filled, gerbil-like mouth. The family was singing "Desperado" by the Eagles and the little girl was trying to keep up with the tune while peppering the back window with corn particles in the process. The little girl responded to Ben's smile with a wave and a smile of her own as the wagon slowly inched by.

"That must be Ben, Dad," the little girl shouted, but Dad told her they would stop and say hello on the way back.

The Winslow family piled out of the station wagon forty yards past Ben's place, where the road ended at the state parking lot. The parking lot was well maintained. It was a direct access point to the lake and the trailhead that winds around North Bay, eventually crossing the Cold River. (This area is known as the Santanoni Reserve.) The trails are well marked and are a favorite excursion for the informed cross-country skier. The Winslows, however, were not as well informed as they were well equipped. Santa had been very good to them this year, cross-country skis for everyone.

Ben had waited until the troop was skiing down the trail before going inside. He enjoyed listening in on the family rhetoric. Clare—that was the little girl's name—was not happy about being separated from her popcorn. She needed to be able to feed the animals along the way, she exclaimed. Her brother, Nolan, solved the problem by helping her fill every pocket and her wool stocking hat with the cheese popcorn; a solution their parents were not aware of.

After adding a log to the woodstove, Ben settled into his chair with a sizable book in hand. There would be time to do a little skiing later, he thought.

His cat, Blacky, took a turn around the chair before curling up at his feet.

Ben had been a champion skier in his prime. He would have made the Olympic team in his day but the times being what they were, just after the war, the Olympics were cancelled. Ben still skied, of course, but when he dreamed it was of himself as a young man skiing. He loved the feeling; that roaring of his internal engine, his head tucked, his ski tips effortlessly driving forward, the wonderment of seeing the world stand still, the looks on the faces in the crowds as he flew by.

Ben awoke to the familiar sound of Erin Prod's Jeep International scraping along Rock Bottom. Fixing his eyes on the clock on the mantel, Ben was not bothered by the fact that he had fallen asleep, it was that he had spent the whole afternoon doing it. While whipping up a batch of hot chocolate, made the old fashioned way with whole milk, Hershey's syrup, and topped off with marshmallows, Ben mumbled, "There goes another day in the fast lane."

Erin, the local Forest Ranger, found that one of the things that helped him sleep at night was that he checked the state parking lots at the end of the day just on the off chance that someone found themselves an unaccounted guest of the land. The habit regularly paid off as each state parking lot is equipped with a registration book. Verifying is merely a matter of referencing the book and any cars still in the lot. He couldn't believe some fools didn't take the time to sign in or out . . . darned flat landers.

Erin and Ben looked forward to their daily harassment of each other. Baseball season had been hard on Erin as he was a Boston Red Sox fan and Ben was for the Yankees, who had made it a pretty one-sided season. Even Erin had to admit when the Yanks swept the World Series the way they did, that they had one of the better teams that year. Now even football season was not going well, with Ben a Minnesota Vikings fan and Erin rooting for the Dallas Cowboys. Lately, Erin had been "crying uncle" early trying to go directly from sports to weather talk and hot chocolate.

Ben, as usual, came out to invite Erin inside. It was snowing hard and obviously had been for some time. Ben beat Erin to the punch, asking if the station wagon was still in the lot. Erin replied with a sullen, "Yea." Ben went on, "Not good. Young family with a little one, probably first time in the Reserve. If you don't take care, a snow like this will cover your tracks in the time it takes to blow your nose. Give me five minutes. I'll grab some things and get my boards."

Erin, a well-experienced outdoorsman, had a great deal of respect for Ben. If there was a family out there in trouble, he would need all the help he could get. He was sure Ben knew the area better than he and that would be a big asset, even if it slowed him down a mite. The onset of exhaustion, dehydration, and hypothermia, the real dangers the Winslows were up against, are often shrugged off or not recognized until it's too late. A chill raced through Erin as he considered the possibility that the family was lost, wet, and in danger.

Ben took the lead. He was wearing a straw basket pack and had a surprisingly quick pace, Erin noticed. He did not ask what Ben had thought to bring in the basket. Ben had won most of the chess games they had played in the past and Erin was willing to leave it at that for now. Erin had his little fanny pack. Inside that was his first aid kit along with the basic staples that would suffice in case of emergency. For now, he thought, Ben's basket pack is not slowing us down any. When Ben's adrenaline rush was over, Erin figured he'd persuade him to leave it alongside the trail.

Darkness fell like a rock, but the fresh snow seemed to illuminate everything it touched. Ben's pace did not change and it was over an hour before he came to a stop. He rinsed his mouth out with water before taking a sip. When Erin caught up to him, Ben handed him the water and began to analyze the situation out loud. Erin could not help but notice Ben was not even winded, while he couldn't stop panting like a basset hound in July.

"I think we have to look at this from the time element point of view," Ben said. "I really don't think they could have gotten that far. They would have had a very poky pace full of rest breaks and snowball fights."

"The storm is letting up and the wind is dying down," Erin interjected. "If you're right and they're still moving, we might get lucky and either cut their tracks or hear them. You know a night like this can carry a voice a long way."

They went another half mile when Ben came to an abrupt stop. He kept looking up the trail and then off to the right. "What's up?" asked Erin.

"Which looks more inviting to you, straight up that hill or down the old creek bed?" Ben asked.

"I see what you're saying," Erin replied, "but the trail is clearly marked right in front of you."

"I see the marker too, but we have the advantage of standing still."

Ben countered thoughtfully, "We know the trail and it's not snowing."

They decided it would be best to split up. Erin would proceed up the trail while Ben played out his hunch. Ben would check it out for a ways and catch up with Erin as soon as possible. When Ben left him, Erin was doing the crab walk up the steep embankment. As he climbed, the forest ranger thought of his brother-in-law, the union plumber, with his conventionally routine schedule; lunches at noon and punching out at five. He paused for a breath; one inhale and the envious feeling was gone. Erin loved his work and he was well-suited for it. "Okay," he thought, "I'm over that hurdle, now if I can just get over this hill."

Ben left his pack at the intersection and was making good time. He was well down the old creek-bed when he noticed a short pine tree along the bank that, like every other tree, was covered with a thick blanket of snow—all except one bough. The bough was holding a good sized pile of popcorn.

Their tracks appeared very faint at first. He started to think about this old stream-bed and then his heart skipped a beat. Not too far off, the stream-bed crossed a good sized beaver flow. It wasn't wide there but very deep and with a strong current that Ben had decided not to test last summer. It had been a very mild winter so far and the ice would be paper-thin. With the fresh snow on it you would not even know the danger.

Ben's heart quickened. His legs pushed harder. "Stretch," he thought. "Use your glide." The tracks were fresh now. "Reach with your arms, push and release the ski. Again, reach, transfer your weight, release." Ben silently shouted to himself, "You must remember to breathe. Breathing is the secret to rhythm and rhythm means speed." The only face present in Ben's mind was that of a certain little curly-haired girl. Once again all the world was standing still while Ben flew.

Little Clare did a classic butt drop into the snow and declared that she would go no further. Mrs. Winslow exchanged a frightened look with her husband. Mr. Winslow, in as confident a tone as he could muster, stated, "It's going to be okay." Nolan continued going on about lions, tigers, and bears.

"Hush," Clare exploded. "I think I hear a tiger or bear coming."

"Come on, Clare, I'll carry you," Mr. Winslow announced. "We haven't got far to go. It looks like it opens up right in front of us. It's probably the main trail. Won't it be funny if we're already back near the car and don't even know it?"

They were just about to step out onto the beaver flow and a wet disaster when in a clear, bellowing voice they heard, "Hold on there!"

Clare rode most of the way back in Ben's basket pack. They had met Erin on the trail; he had doubled back figuring something was up when Ben had not returned.

When they made it back to Ben's place, six choruses of "Desperado" later, they enjoyed a good cheeseburger dinner with plenty of hot chocolate. Erin listened to Nolan's lecture on how to handle lions, tigers, and bears in difficult situations. Clare found the most comfortable spot in the house and fell asleep. Of course that spot was Ben's lap, in front of the fire, holding Blacky the cat.

That night, long after all had left, Ben slept. He dreamed of skiing in his own backyard, as well as in far off places. The champion skier in his dreams was the same man that he would find in the morning when he awoke.

CABIN FEVER

For Ma and Uncle, every morning started about
the same. At sunup (without the aid of an alarm
clock I might add), the two would meet and share a
large pot of black coffee. They liked sitting in front
of the picture window, not really doing much talking unless it was to grunt or groan over the crack-
ing of a joint. When something was said it was always short, abrupt, and to the point. They had a
close friendship and knew each other so well that
they needed no frills and lace when they spoke to
each other.

This particular morning, during Ma's second

cup of coffee, she said, "It's going to be a long winter. Folks know it already. I think we need a little jab of excitement around here. Don't want anyone to go batty on us this winter." Uncle replied with a short hum. The two sat in comfortable silence until the pot of coffee was finished and the morning sun's rays filled the window.

Mid-January in Tavern's Corner and the snowbanks were already chest high. It was shaping up to be a very long, cold, snowy winter. Folks were getting an early touch of cabin fever. An added cause to the mid-winter grumps was that football season was almost over. The end of football season was like a national emergency all-points bulletin that read, "Don't go outside. Grab the women and children. Shut the doors and board up the windows. Old Man Winter is loose, and pillaging small villages."

It was a typical Sunday at the Tavern House. The usual crowd was there. It was one week before the Super Bowl and there wasn't much to do but sit around and talk about football. Jed and Nesy were arguing with Earl and Luke.

"Sure the Denver Broncos put a tramping on everyone in the past, but their day is over. Elway is long gone and Terrell Davis may never really recover from that knee injury," Earl said.

Nesy jumped in by saying, "Terrell Davis is in his prime, and the best running back there is."

Luke shouted back, "Elway was such a pretty boy! If I was surrounded by all those superstars, Terrell, Ed Mcaffrey, and Shannon Sharpe, I could have led the Bronco's to those Bowls myself."

"You," said Jed, "can't even flip a flapjack let alone throw a football while a thousand pounds of meat charges at you trying to rip your heart out."

Well, one thing led to another. Someone made the comparison of Luke's nose to the old busted muffler that had been leaning against the building for the past year. Luke referred to Jed's sometime slight limp as the Walter Brennan shuffle, calling him, "Gramps." Earl had just referred to Nesy as Mr. Marlin Perkins from "Mutual of Omaha's Wild Kingdom."

Suddenly, out of nowhere, a football came crashing down on the table. The crash knocked beers over which spilled onto unguarded laps. It also spun the ashtray into the air, doing a triple-flip, flinging ashes everywhere. Uncle had gotten their undivided attention. He then said, "Ma, get me my coat. You boys outside, I'm refereeing."

"What?" said Nesy. "There's got to be two feet of snow on the ground!" Someone made a cat-like meow. Jed pushed Luke. Uncle once again said in a clear tone, "Outside."

Jed and Nesy won the coin toss. The front yard of the Tavern House was about fifty by forty feet and served as a snow-covered playing field. It was a sunny day. Uncle was snug in his rocker on the front porch with a blanket over his lap. Nesy was quarterbacking and had just completed a couple of short passes to Jed. They were soon within scoring position. There had been others inside the Tavern House who had drifted out onto the porch to watch the fun, one of whom was Erin Prod. Jed had just caught the ball and was plowing through the snow running parallel to the porch. Jed was almost to the supposed end zone when Erin leaped from the porch, giving Jed a perfect blind side shoulder tackle. When Erin rose you could see Jed was pile-driven to the bottom of the snow bank at the end of the porch. Rich Parker had also been inside the Tavern House that morning and needed no encouragement to join in and even the sides. The game was well underway when the Robinson family came into town. They were a large family with five boys and two girls. They came to the Tavern House on Sundays for the lunch specials and to read the latest magazines: *Agricultural, Farm and Garden, Country Living, Sweet Sixteen,* and the *National Inquirer.* Old man Robinson was at times referred to as Mr. Ebenezer, from Dickens' *Christmas Carol*. He was often heard ridiculing anyone who was willing to degrade himself by actually purchasing a frivolous thing such as a magazine as he buried his head in the *Inquirer*. With a consenting nod from Mrs. Robinson and a little grumbling from Mr. Robinson the "children" joined in on the fun.

Luke and Earl's team was a little bigger and was starting to dominate what was later referred to as the second quarter. Fatalities were still relatively low. Nesy had a little trickle of blood coming from his nose. Rick Parker had lost one of his false teeth. But things evened up once again when Dave Cocker joined Jed and Nesy's team.

By this time, the front porch was full of spectators. The news of the game was spreading fast. Folks were coming from all over to see the fun. Ma was cursing up a storm as she tried to keep up with the food and drink orders. It wasn't long before Ma was shouting, "If you know where it is, get it yourself!"

The game lasted till dark. Although no one really knew what the score was, both teams claimed they were still in the lead. In what ended up being the last play of the game, Luke and Earl tried the old Statue of Liberty play. Luke was quarterbacking and called the play from the huddle. Luke told the

Robinsons to "go with a tight flying wedge and mow everything down in your path." (As a reader, you should know that this play and formation is now illegal in the pros for humanitarian reasons.) Luke told Earl, "I'll step back and fake the pass. I'll pose like a morning buck. Earl, you swing behind nonchalantly and take the ball from my hand." All in all, it was a proven play in many backyard games.

The only problem was that Nesy had taken many a bruise as a youngster, being a last-picked sub in a backyard game. Nesy recognized the play right away. When Luke reached way back with his arm as if to pass it wasn't Earl who took the ball from his hand, it was Nesy. Nesy broke several tackles from the Robinson girl, who clung to him as he ran for the touchdown.

As Nesy reached the end zone, simultaneously there was a loud bang. It was Uncle. He was standing up holding his .30-06 rifle. As loud as he could Uncle shouted, "All the drinks and food you can hold—it's on Ma." Just then the most brutal shot of the day was given. Old Ma gave Uncle her best Mohammed Ali punch right to the kidneys!

THE WITCH OF TUPPER LAKE

On a warm day in early February, Nesy ate breakfast at the Tavern House, scrambled eggs and ham. Nancy had not come with him this weekend and he missed her, some sort of office deadline thing. The two of them had been coming up each weekend for most of the winter. They were having fun fixing up the Old Mill House, their home away from home. The husband and wife-bonding thing had been going very well.

Nesy's heart just wasn't into it today. He took his time with breakfast, reading an old *Field and Stream* magazine as he ate. Jed quietly planted himself in the chair across from Nesy. He held a huge cup of hot chocolate filled with those floating little marshmallows. Nesy did not even realize Jed was there until Jed whispered, "Let's go fishing."

"Fishing," Nesy said. "What are you talking about?"

"Ice fishing. It's not like a usual day at the river, but at least its fishing," Jed explained. "We'll go over to Tupper Lake and jig for lakers. It's pretty wild pulling a thirty-inch lake trout through an eight-inch hole in the ice. It's a warm day, not much wind, a couple of lounge chairs and a big lunch. Uncle told me the other day that it's time to hit North Bay. The big six to eight pounders tend to yard up just about two hundred feet off shore." Jed lowered his voice to a whisper. "My truck is all loaded. All we have left to do is raid Ma's kitchen for lunch."

They were just pulling their heads out of Ma's big double refrigerator, with four arms full—half a ham, four turkey legs, hard boiled eggs, and some sort of raisin cake thing with white icing—when they heard a low purr-like noise. They froze, then turned their heads slowly. It was Ma. She was in a low crouched position like an African cat ready to pounce. You could see the look of fear in Jed and Nesy's eyes. Ma was holding her broom so tight you could hear it squeak under her grip as her knuckles whitened. Jed smiled his best smile saying, "Now Ma, this stuff would probably have spoiled anyway. Think of the time and trouble we've saved you, the mess and smell and all. You could say we saved you a lot of bother and work." All was quiet. Ma kinda straightened up, giving her little frownlike smile. Then the boys relaxed, straightened up, and started to laugh. In doing so they took their eyes off Ma just for a second. That was a big mistake.

They were still choking on straw bristles from Ma's broom as they loaded the groceries into the car. Uncle came out, "I see by the amount of straw in your hair and what's covering your clothes, Ma fixed you lunch."

Uncle advised them to use a silver Swedish spoon and to bounce it off the bottom of the lake. Uncle started to walk away after saying good luck but turned back quickly and pointed a finger at Jed.

"Don't forget, stay away from Pine Point and that witch's house. You never know what that woman's up to; or what she'll be able to get you to do. If she does come up on you, I wouldn't mention my name," Uncle said.

The boys were laughing as they left, promising to bring back lake trout fillets for dinner tonight.

Nesy smiled mockingly, "Uncle and his stories, 'The Witch of Tupper Lake'."

Uncle walked back to the Tavern House, but hesitated on the porch. He looked up at the sky, then at the thermometer on the front window casing. "I wish I had remembered to tell them to watch themselves crossing the barren straight." (That's the nickname for the fault line where North Bay meets the main channel.) "On a day like today that can practically be open water," Uncle muttered to himself. "But they're smart boys."

Uncle then went directly to the kitchen and told Ma she should make a big pot of vegetable noodle soup this afternoon.

Jed neglected to mention to Nesy that a mile or so walk was involved. The usual daily supplies for ice fishermen weighed them down. In Jed's mind, this was just a quick jaunt, as if he were fishing alongside the car. Packing the gear demanded little thought. Squeezing lounge chairs under their arms and basket packs filled with fishing gear, food, more food, and beer on their backs, they set off across the ice.

"This isn't much different than a day at Jones Beach in the city," Nesy thought as he bounced on his toes to re-grip his load. God, he always dreaded that endless walk from the parking lot to the beach. The ice today reflected a hard glare from the sun. Nesy walked only two steps behind Jed, his eyes half-closed against the sun. He was enjoying its warmth. Nesy suddenly heard Jed say something and then it sounded as though Jed had dropped his pack and in doing so broke all the dishes. Nesy's eyes opened wide with sudden realization. They hadn't brought any dishes.

Jed was treading water, trying to belly his way back onto the ice. Nesy's foot was right there in front of him. Jed was able to get a finger grip on Nesy's ankle. He hollered at Nesy to sit down. Nesy stood there wearing a smirk, looking down at Jed. "Well Mr. Adirondack Mountain Man," he thought. Again Nesy heard the loud sound of dishes breaking. Now it was Jed's turn to smile. The ice once again broke apart. This time Nesy plunged into the water.

They had quite a time crawling out, Nesy being the first by crawling up and over Jed. Jed finally got out by hanging onto one end of a lounge chair while Nesy tugged on the other end.

For a moment the two stood looking around and shivering. Their things that hadn't sunk were strewn about. The slight breeze that seemed refreshing on the walk in was now bone piercing cold. Nesy noticed it first; smoke. It was coming from the woods not more than three hundred yards away. The two exchanged quick glances followed by a nod of their heads. They walked the short distance cautiously, the smell of delicious home baking drew them to the dwelling.

"You don't suppose this is the witch's house Uncle warned us about," Nesy whispered. Jed did not answer. Before them sat a small cabin snuggly placed in a clearing of pines. The boys walked onto the porch, listening intently. The door opened suddenly and a woman, already turning away, said over her shoulder, "Come on in. I saw you out there on the ice. There are blankets on the chair next to the fire."

The boys did so, hesitantly at first, but they soon overcame their reluctance aided by the smell of fresh apple pie and the warmth of the room. The fire was crackling and the two were drawn across the room to the heat. Again they heard the woman's voice coming from another room. "I hope you like venison stew and apple pie, I think there is plenty," she said.

"Did you get a look at her?" Nesy asked Jed. Jed shook his head and Nesy added, "Me neither, but why am I reminded of the story of Hansel and Gretel?"

The voice came closer now. She came into the

room carrying a fairly large black kettle, one hand on the handle and the other hand supporting it from below. The fact that the pot hid her face drew the boys unconsciously to the edge of their seats. She bent over and placed the pot on the iron hook, swinging the pot so it hung over the fire. She stayed in that bent position stirring the pot. The boys were in chairs on opposite sides of both the fire and her. It was the first chance they'd had to get a look at her.

Nesy couldn't believe his eyes. She was the most beautiful woman he had ever seen. It was hard to get a really good look at her though. The steam from the pot and the smoke coming from the fire kept sweeping across her face. Nesy kept blinking his eyes as if to clear the mist. He could see that she had strawberry blonde hair, wore very little makeup, and had a small beauty mark on her right cheek. As she turned her head a little his way and smiled, he realized that his pulse was racing. He slowly sat back in his chair, not wanting to give the impression that he was staring.

Jed had also been waiting for his chance to look at the witch of Tupper Lake. As she stirred the pot her back was slightly turned his way, making it impossible for him to see her face. On the other hand he was able to see Nesy's face. Judging by

Nesy's reaction, he thought she must truly be a homely, haggard thing. She shifted her feet, it was obviously an uncomfortable position to be in.

"I think it just needs to simmer a little, boys," she said. "I've got to go check on the apple pie. You boys are lucky. The apple barrel was almost empty."

While talking, she had moved so that her back was now facing Nesy. It was Jed's turn to get a look at the old witch.

Jed was stunned. She had jet-black hair and eyes that sparkled from deep within. The steam from the pot was rising and the smoke and the shadows made by the fire made it hard to get a good look. It was like looking at a slightly out of focus picture. She looked his way and smiled. Jed was breathing so hard through his nose that he reminded Nesy of the big bull they had seen last summer at the state fair.

The fire crackled and at the same time the woman abruptly stood up and walked out of the room. The boys could hear her singing, "Puff the Magic Dragon" from the kitchen. Jed and Nesy were busy with their own thoughts, pondering what a sweet, sexy voice she had. Funny that they hadn't realized it before.

Nesy broke the silence. "My God, she's the most

beautiful woman I've ever seen. Wait until I see Uncle. That was a pretty mean trick he pulled on us with that old witch story."

Just as Nesy finished his statement, the loud crash of a pot hitting the floor was heard from the kitchen. Jed had been staring transfixed into the fire. The clatter awakened him. "Did you look into her eyes," Jed said, shaking his head. "I think I know what they mean by love at first sight."

"You boys better be getting out of those wet things. There's no need to be so bashful," the voice called out from the kitchen.

Standing around in their red flannel long johns, Jed's a little worse for wear, he muttered, "Dang, I think my toe's frozen again. It always gives me trouble since I got frostbitten six or seven years ago." He went on to say, "I suppose one of us should consider gathering up whatever stuff might be left out on the ice."

It took Nesy a minute to catch on, "You're not trying to get rid of me are you, so you can stay here and make some brownie points?"

The silky voice from the kitchen spoke again. "You boys better throw some more wood on the fire. Don't even give a second thought about the wood-bin being low. I've been meaning to fill it, I'll get it later."

Jed and Nesy insisted on spending the next two hours filling the wood bin, shoveling a path to the wood stack at the back of the house, and stacking two cords of wood on the side porch. The boys never saw their host, but every once in a while they would see a curtain move or hear a remark. "Look at those muscles," she'd say. "Jed, you must lift weights. Nesy, look how efficient you are. Every stick of wood is stacked perfectly." It didn't seem to matter to Jed and Nesy that they were sweating so hard that once again they were drenched from head to toe.

When they entered the house, coughing and dripping, they heard the woman's voice sing out, "I'm in the pantry." The way her silky voice floated into the room reminded the boys instantly of their host's beauty. "Either of you boys know how to grease a pump like the one in my kitchen? You'll have to talk me through it so I can give it a try later," she said.

The boys needed no encouragement. They were soon at work on the pump. After a time, with Nesy buried from the waist up under the sink, Jed snuck into the pantry. It was very dark. "Are you in here?" he whispered. The woman replied with a yes. "I can't see you," Jed said.

"It will take a while for your eyes to adjust. The

lamp just ran out of oil," her voice said. Jed could hear her coming closer. "You're a scoundrel," she said, giving him a light quick kiss on the cheek. She was out the door seconds later. Jed returned to helping Nesy with the pump. He was also thinking what a tough life it was out here alone like this. Must be hard on a woman. He touched his cheek and smiled. Strangely, her lips felt a little rough, though her allure made it hard to notice. An hour later the men were of course still exhausted, dripping with sweat and now covered with grease.

"Hey boys," the woman said, "I think this stew is just about perfect." The boys entered the living room as the side door was closing. "I'm out here letting this pot cool for a minute. I wanted to clean out the hearth and chimney before we eat anyway. After dinner maybe we should heat some water for bathing." The boys' heads turned simultaneously, staring. A huge ivory white tub gleamed along the wall.

The boys were exhausted, dripping with sweat, covered with grease, and now blanketed with soot.

The room was quiet as they waited for their host to return. Nesy rubbed his nose with the back of his hand. He had tried to find a clean spot on his hand but failed. Then he just stood there, looking himself up and down. He felt as if he had just found out he had caught an infectious disease. Watching Nesy, Jed started to laugh. As he did so, he started to assess his own looks and realized he was no better off. The two of them stared at each other. They were soon laughing uncontrollably.

Jed noticed first, "Our clothes are gone!" The two walked out on the porch to tell their host they needed to clean up for dinner and to ask where she had put their clothes.

Except for the pot with its lid in place, the porch was empty. Their host was nowhere to be found. Nesy leaned over and lifted the lid, but the pot was empty and stone cold. The door suddenly slammed shut behind them.

"Hey, just what's going on!" Jed hollered. "What kind of game are we playing!" No reply.

Nesy knocked on the door saying, "Okay now, that's very funny, let us in."

Standing on the porch, the boys noticed the curtains were slowly being drawn open and sunlight filled the window. As the window slowly lifted open, they stepped closer. An old woman's face abruptly appeared at the open window. Her well-wrinkled face was surrounded by long, coarse, white hair. A large mole sprouting a clump of hair clung to her right cheek. A small whitish mustache covered her upper lip. Jed rubbed his cheek.

The old woman started to speak, but was stopped by a coughing fit. She cleared her throat and again the boys heard the same sweet silky voice they had been listening to all day. They shuddered. "Now boys," she said, "it's getting late and if you stay along the shoreline and go right back to your car you'll make it before dark. You be sure to tell Uncle he should have made an honest woman of me years ago like he had promised. Mind you it's not too late." In a more stern voice the woman said, "Now you best go." With a wink of her eye she added, "Of course, Jed, you are welcome to come calling again." She puckered up her lips and blew a kiss as she closed the window.

Jed and Nesy had a hard time coming up with a plausible story at the Tavern House. After all, they returned in quite a state, wearing nothing but their trashed long johns and boots. As far as the witch of Tupper Lake goes, the encounter was not mentioned.

Jed and Nesy pacified their minds by agreeing that there were actually two women. One, an old woman who carried some sort of grudge towards Uncle—she had probably overheard the boys mention his name—and a young woman, perhaps her daughter, who helped her carry out her scheme.

They never did agree on the looks of the

younger woman.

Uncle still lets Jed and Nesy know when the ice fishing at Tupper Lake is apt to be good. The boys, however, always seem to be a little too occupied elsewhere to make it over there.

THE WOODSMAN

Nesy and Nancy were sitting on the porch of the Tavern House, sipping wine and enjoying the warmth of the late evening breeze. Spring had been a long time coming. Here and there you could see mist rising from patches of snow. The Tavern House didn't have much of a wine cellar nor a connoisseur to recommend what would be best suited to accompany pheasant a l'orange. In fact, the whole wine list consisted of a large bottle of Chianti kept behind the bar. Ma liked to look at the bottle, the extra long thin neck and the straw basket that encased the bottom of the bottle. She said it added a sense of worldly culture to the place.

Nancy was talking about the contrast between yellow wallpaper in the kitchen and the light blue paper she wanted to put up in the hallway back at the Mill House. Nesy was only half listening, yet he was staring at her as if trying to memorize her face. Now Nancy wasn't one to drivel on and on with boring rhetoric. She was a far better conversationalist than most, including Nesy, whether talking politics, world economics, baseball, or the imminent care needed for a newborn child. She was well educated and had a good sense for applied logic. Nancy had a way that drew people to her to talk about most anything. It was true, even here in the middle of the Adirondacks. It's not that Nesy was bored. He was thinking how much he loved her and wondering how he had gotten so lucky.

Nesy was still pleasantly grinning when Erin Prod came out of the Tavern House, apparently talking to a fellow Forest Ranger.

"We'll have to get an early start tomorrow, although I haven't quite made up my mind exactly where we'll start," Erin said. "The information we have to go on from these two college kids is pretty sketchy. It's always amazing to me how people can go into the woods without using a lick of common sense."

"Just what do we have to go on?" Erin's colleague asked.

"Well," Erin said, "practically nothing except where they left their car before they went into the woods over near the west bank of Giant Mountain. They made it to the lookout point on top of Giant and decided to find a different way down. Of course they had no compass, no food, no water, and get this, the kid who's lost is wearing shorts, a blue T-shirt, and sneakers. He's lucky it's a warm night tonight. If he stays put maybe we'll be able to get him out tomorrow before the cold snap comes in." Erin went on, "The kids say that they wound up in a thick pine forest that blotted out the sky. It was probably young stuff because at times they said they had to get down on their hands and knees and try to swim their way through. They got pretty cut up and disoriented. They don't even know exactly when they noticed their friend was missing. He was the only one wearing a watch."

The fellow ranger was shaking his head. Erin continued, "They finally came out of the thick stuff near some waterfalls. The girl rested there for a while, curled up in the roots of some big tree, while the other kid yelled, trying to locate their other companion. By then they were both probably in a state of shock. They somehow finally wandered out to the highway. Some trucker picked them up and they landed on my doorstep about forty minutes ago. I was hoping Uncle would be able to give us his thoughts on where this guy could have ended up. I think he, the local guru, knows every rock and tree around here by first name. He's off with Jed, his nephew, to some antique car show down in Lake George for the weekend."

The rangers walked off the porch saying, "You know how many streams there are this time of year coming off these mountains? It will be pitch black in another thirty minutes and I'm not about to risk somebody else getting lost or hurt. We'll get an early start before sun up. He'll just have to keep."

Next Nesy heard, Nancy was saying something about separate checkbooks and perhaps beds to match. Nesy blinked his eyes and linked, "Uh huh," with a long, "What?!?"

Nancy laughed, saying, "Come on handsome. Walk me home."

Nancy got an early start the next morning, scraping off the old wallpaper in the hallway. Nesy was puttering around the kitchen making coffee. He had trouble sleeping during the night. His mind kept wandering back to the conversation he had overheard from Erin and the other ranger. To make coffee for two, Nesy should have put five teaspoons of granulated beans into the coffee maker. On the ninth tablespoon Nesy said out loud, "Of course." It was the description of the area the hikers had given that kept bothering Nesy. Thick pines, the sky being blotted out, on your hands and knees as if swimming through, coming out near a waterfall, a tree with roots large enough to curl up in. It sounded just like the area Nesy had gotten lost in the first day he'd arrived at Taverns Corner.

"Honey, I have to run a little errand, won't be too long," said Nesy.

That drew Nancy to the kitchen. "What's up? Sounds like a ditch to me."

"There is a guy lost in the woods, and believe it or not, I think I know just where he is."

"You're not taking a fishing pole with you by any chance, are you?" Nancy asked.

Nesy told Nancy about the conversation he had overheard and the fact that the kid had been out there overnight. "I know it's a long shot. I wouldn't be able to explain to someone without them laughing. They'd tell me there are a lot of pine trees in the Adirondacks, not to mention spring creeks and large trees with roots. I can't explain it, but something tells me that I know where this kid is."

A few minutes later Nesy was out the door with a daypack over his shoulder. He was an educated country boy now. His pack was not bulky. It had all of the things a local boy took for granted. The things anyone with an ounce of woods sense wouldn't leave the yard without. Now, a businessman wouldn't leave the house without his brief case. Inside it he would have his daily planner, with a monthly calendar. He would have note-paper, pens and pencils, a bunch of folders filled with current projects, maybe a pocket dictionary, and a calculator. It's just ordinary common sense. Nesy's pack held a local topographical map, a compass, a water bottle, a flashlight, extra jack knife, a rolled up long sleeved polo shirt, matches, and of course, the all important toilet paper. Everything was sealed in water-tight ziplock bags. The only variable for a woodsman is which snacks or sandwiches he'll throw in just before leaving. Hopefully, this wasn't when he realized he had left an uneaten pastrami-on-rye-with-mustard sandwich in from the last time.

Nancy followed him onto the porch carrying her cup of coffee. She kissed his cheek and sternly told him to be careful. She waved good-bye and took what ended up being quite an eye-opening sip of coffee.

The old stump road was well named. Nesy's Range Rover was none the worse for wear mechanically but the back country town roads had taken care of the once glossy red paint job with their many overhanging branches and downfallen trees. Nesy drove as far as he could and then some. He left the vehicle standing like a three-legged dog.

Nesy knew exactly where he was going but took a compass reading anyway. Soon he was alongside the stream he had once followed into the woods. In no time at all he was at the waterfall and pool. It only took a couple of minutes to find the huge pine tree that he had once taken comfort in, lying among the hammock-like roots. The area was covered with a thick blanket of pine needles. It looked undisturbed. Nesy was just about to sit down when he spotted something on the ground not too far off, a red bandana.

Nesy took another compass reading before going any further. Before him was an imaginary border. Crossing it would be like entering a dimly lit world. The huge mazelike thick pine forest was before him. He had no real longing to enter.

After an hour of walking and crawling around, looking for any signs and listening for any responses to his shouts, Nesy was ready to give up. He was sitting in what would be the closest thing to a clearing in the area, thinking, "If I was lost and right here, what would I do?"

This thought made him check his compass for the twentieth time. He stood up and put his compass back in his pocket. While doing so he noticed a large branch leaning against a good sized tree right before him. It was the placement of the branch that seemed so odd. It made kind of a perfect ladder, that is, if you had a reason to climb such a tree.

This is a stupid idea, Nesy was thinking while he balanced himself before reaching for a better hold. If I fall, I wonder if I'd bounce or just imbed myself a foot into the ground. Once in the tree, Nesy noticed several places where it looked like bark had been torn off. Nesy was talking out loud to himself, "Now, if I was lost and climbed this tree . . ." In only one direction was there any real view and that was of the ridge of what happened to be the nearest mountain. Nesy took another compass reading. Looking at the ridge he smiled—high ground, good boy.

He was on top of the ridge in no time at all. He had been hollering just about every hundred yards, but had gotten no reply. Once on top of the rocky bald ridge, Nesy sat down. The lost hiker surely would have come this far, but now what? Nesy was just about to holler one more time. He was taking a deep breath in order to make a good effort, when a voice not more than fifteen feet away, very low said, "I'm over here." The boy was lying down, actually stuffed into a good-sized crevasse and an oblong, waist-high boulder looked like it was resting on top of him.

Nesy could see the young man had recently been crying. Trying to put him at ease, Nesy commented, "I heard tell of guys like you who like to rough it. I prefer a blanket myself."

The youth explained in short verse, "I don't think I'm really hurt. I was lost. I came up here thinking maybe I'd see a house or a road. I was standing on top of this rock, when...well, it rolled over! Next thing I knew, I was pinned down here. I tried to get it off me, I pushed and pushed."

Nesy cut in, afraid the young man would get hysterical. "You're not going to believe this, but the same thing happened to a friend of mine several times. Now he won't even take his dog for a walk without taking a hammer and chisel." The two of them shared the laugh. "I have got to get something to use as a lever. I'll be back before you can sing Charlie Daniels' 'The Devil Went Down to Georgia.' "

"I don't know that one," the young man replied, "nor 'Possum up a Gumtree.' Can you get this rock off me or not?"

The size of the rock was misleading, for it was

nowhere near as heavy as it looked. Nesy, with the aid of a good sturdy oak branch, was able to flip the rock over and off the kid on the first try. The young man, hesitantly at first, crawled out of the crevasse. He shook one limb and then the other. Soon he was bouncing around with excitement like a genie released from a bottle. Nesy grinned.

The boy came to a sudden halt. He turned to Nesy, "You do know your way out of here, right? How far is the nearest anything?"

"Relax," Nesy told the young man. "We're about two hours from my car. Here, put this shirt on and drink some water. We'll eat some sandwiches once we get off this ridge and out of the wind."

Nesy was just about pulling up to the Tavern House. The young man had fallen asleep, practically as soon as he hit the passenger's seat. Nesy had been savoring in his mind what it would be like once inside the tavern room. The pats on the back, the amazement on their faces, everyone wanting to hear every detail. Nesy pulled up to the front walk. He reached over and lightly shook the boy saying, "We're here! I'm sure you'll find your friends inside." The young man bolted from the car towards the tavern without even shutting the door. Nesy had to reach over to close it. Doing so, he whispered, "Its been nice meeting you, young man."

Nesy looked at the Tavern House again. He didn't notice it before, but Uncle was sitting in his rocker on the porch smoking his pipe. Uncle raised his hand slowly, giving a short wave, a smile, and a tip of the hat. Nesy replied with a wave of his own, just before driving off.

Afterword

The Adirondack Mountains are some of the oldest mountains in the world. The Rockies, Andes, and even the Alps, with their tall points and sharp edges, are children in comparison. Time has treaded many years on the Adirondacks, wearing them down, and leaving behind many unnamed mountains, lost ponds, and unusual mountain valleys. If you get the chance, you should come and take a look for yourself. You can always stop at Tavern's Corner and share the fireplace with Uncle, or catch Jed and Nesy's latest adventure. Just be careful—if you should ask for directions and decide to talk a little baseball.

To Scott
Within our hearts,
as within this book,
is a large part of you.

About the Author

Dan Gillman was born and raised in the Adirondacks where he now resides with his wife, Julie. There the two are raising a brood of their own, passing on the same values and local lore only the Adirondacks can offer. Gillman comes from a typical middle class family. In his childhood there were not summer family trips to Europe or Colorado. Instead, Gillman grew up learning to appreciate the heritage of the area around him, the Adirondacks. He is presently an area businessman, but had always aspired to be a professional athlete. He says his only shortcomings in that pursuit have been due to his own athletic ability. Now, somewhat over the hill, he spends most of his free time exploring the countless rivers, mountains, and lakes of the Adirondacks, usually accompanied by his fly fishing pole. He has heard many a tale along the way and has shared the colors of the trees and the lives of the people who reside there.